MEET FINNY ALETTER...

She's brainy and beautiful, an accomplished
wizard in the cutthroat, big-money world of
stocks and bonds. On the fast track to success,
she swims with the sharks, battles corporate
predators—and unravels tangled blood knots
of greed, mayhem...and murder!

SCAVENGERS

SCAVENGERS

YVONNE MONTGOMERY

AVON BOOKS ◆ NEW YORK

AVON BOOKS
A division of
The Hearst Corporation
105 Madison Avenue
New York, New York 10016

Copyright © 1987 by Yvonne Ewegen
Published by arrangement with Arbor House/William Morrow and
Company, Inc.
Library of Congress Catalog Card Number: 86-32165
ISBN: 0-380-71002-1

First Avon Books Printing: August 1990

AVON TRADEMARK REG. U.S. PAT. OFF. AND IN OTHER COUNTRIES, MARCA
REGISTRADA, HECHO EN U.S.A.

Printed in the U.S.A.

RA 10 9 8 7 6 5 4 3 2 1

For Bob, Misty, and Shane:
You made it possible

ACKNOWLEDGMENTS

I am grateful to the following people who read and commented upon this work in progress: Martha and John Birney, Enid and Tom Schantz, Judy Brimberg, Linda Roberts, Midge Pierce, and Barbara Carbutt. For their unfailing love and support, special thanks go to Betsy Cox, Sandi Kristen Olsen, and my parents, Floyd and Mildred Montgomery.

Thanks to my editor, Liza Dawson, and her assistant, Sarah Williamson, for all they've done to make this book better. Finally, my love and gratitude go to Larry and Lynne Block, who taught me how to write for my life.

SCAVENGERS

CHAPTER

I

*D*enver was shutting down for the night. It was a sprawling, land-locked ocean of a city, its waves of houses splashing up onto the foothills of the Rocky Mountains. At its center was a jagged skyline of new and unfinished high rises.

On the streets below, the daytime activity ebbed as the city's workers withdrew to the suburbs. In the few unrenewed corners of the city, the winos and transients began to gather in the night, flotsam left behind.

A ragpicker pushed a shopping cart through an alley, stopping to poke through the contents of a rusted dumpster. A cold wind pushed an open newspaper against his legs. When he swung about to kick it loose light from a window across the alley illuminated his face. It was as stark as a wooden mask, motionless except for the eyes that burned with enraged isolation.

1

His eyes met those of the woman standing at the window of the renovated two-story brick house. He stood his ground, glaring hatred.

Finny Aletter let the heavy curtain drop and turned quickly from the window. She shivered and sipped from the small snifter in her hand. Amaretto slid warmly down her throat. She tried to push the image of the creature in the alley out of her mind.

The telephone shrieked into the silence, and she jogged through the unfinished dining room into the living room. Her jeans had bled from blue to gray, and her stained T-shirt proclaimed "Beauty Fades With Time, But Dumb Is Forever."

She pushed aside the jumble of used sandpaper on the round oak coffee table and scooped up the receiver. "Hello." She sank back into the brown corduroy sofa.

"Finny, so glad I caught you at home."

"Greg." The alert humor that characterized Finny's face smoothed into an expressionless mask.

"I wanted to congratulate you for the first-rate job you did on the Barchester account this morning. I didn't have a chance to let you know how impressed I was."

You were too busy sucking up to their staff people, Finny thought. "Thank you."

"I know the brass were practically swinging from the chandeliers. Elliot told me how proud he is of you."

Ah, one-upmanship. Finny could just see Greg, the beach-boy blondness, steadfast hazel eyes that hid the instincts of a cut-rate Machiavelli and the morals of a shark.

"He told me, too."

"That's what I heard."

Finny closed her eyes. God bless the grapevine. Elliot had noted the signing of the Barchester Mutual Fund with Lakin & Fulton this morning by walking their new clients out of the office, then coming back to catch Finny up in a fierce hug, kissing both her cheeks, then her mouth. He'd pulled out of the kiss to look into her eyes, then kissed her again, putting some body English into it that came straight out of old times but had no business being there now.

"—isn't all that much of a disadvantage, being a woman, is it?" Greg was overdoing the tone of rueful camaraderie. His chuckle crawled over the telephone wire. "Elliot never came on to me for buttoning up an account."

"You're not his type." Finny dropped the phone receiver onto its cradle. If Greg knew about this morning, then it would be served up with the coffee and Danish at Lakin & Fulton tomorrow morning.

"Hell." Finny pried herself out of the sofa and retrieved her glass from the welter of tools on the table. "More booze," she muttered, crunching her way through the brittle curls of white paint that littered the floor.

"God, what a mess." Finny grabbed the bottle that held pride of place on the newly stripped mantel and poured generously into the small balloon of a glass. The nut-brown liqueur shimmered in the beveled mirror above the fireplace.

She caught sight of herself as she lifted the glass to her lips, and a nasty grin split her face. Smudges on both cheeks, paint chips making her short black hair prematurely gray—hell, even her hands looked like Cinderella's after prolonged overtime. If only Greg could see her now. It almost would be worth putting up with his repellent presence. He'd have a hell of a time painting her as the office seductress.

"He wouldn't even know who I was," she said into the comfortable silence of the room. Her smile died. She would have to deal with whatever mischief Greg decided to make. Probably more in the vein he'd already mined: filling Colter Lakin's head with stories of her supposed sexual activities with an assortment of staff people. He'd had some success with that line already, aided in part by the bruises Colter's ego had sustained when she'd found his advances resistible.

Colter wouldn't care that she had nailed down the biggest deal of her career. No, consummated—that would be the word he'd use. No one had ever known Colter Lakin to pass up an opportunity for sexual innuendo. Entering his sixties had given him a new lease on lust.

Finny drained her glass and thumped it onto the mantel. No doubt about it, she was sick of her job. Burnout or creeping good taste had soured her on market machinations, and there were enough women account executives around now so that the liberation flag had flagged. She had run like hell to jump on the bandwagon—only to figure out that it was going in the wrong direction.

The shelves next to the fireplace held the stereo equipment, and she rifled randomly through the stacks of tapes. She slid a cassette into the tape deck, and the overblown rapture of Rachmaninoff unfurled across the room.

Finny began sweeping up the paint chips. Her eyes flicked over the mantel as she pushed the growing pile of chips from one place to another. It looked good. She could apply a coat of paint remover to get up the last of the residue and it would be ready for sanding tomorrow night.

She reached out to run her fingertips over the garland of flowers that had been artfully carved into the frontispiece of the mantel. Oak buttercups. She'd had to use a nutpick with the heat gun to get the paint out of the tiny crevices between the petals. Doing it had made her happier than signing the Barchester Mutual Fund.

Finny bulldozed the pile of paint chips to the base of the fireplace and propped the broom against the mantel. The mouth of the Amaretto bottle found its way to the mouth of her glass.

She was going to have to quit her job.

The half-serious suggestion from the carpenter who had replaced the balusters on her stairs had been nothing more than an audible expression of an idea that had been playing hide-and-seek inside her for several years. "You ever want to get into restoration seriously, give me a call. You do good work."

Finny's smile slipped. How would her mother adjust to going from My Unmarried Daughter the Stockbroker to My Still Unmarried Daughter the Carpenter? At thirty-six it was practically required that she have a mid-life crisis, right?

The doorbell rang. Finny glanced at her watch: It was after eight. She looked around the wreck of the living room and cursed under her breath. The bell rang again. "Coming," she yelled and ran quickly across the floor.

The shadow of a woman slid across the frosted oval window in the door as Finny pulled it open. "Julia," she said, surprised.

Julia Simons stood in the glare of the porch light, a manila folder clasped in both hands. Her light brown hair was swept into a loose knot of curls, artful tendrils escaping down both sides, and her eyes were carefully made up. The stylish lines of her beige coat made her look like a child playing dress-up.

Julia burst into speech. "I'm sorry to be so late with this, but Elliot wanted to leave early and I had to do his work first, of course. I hurried as fast as I could."

Finny took the folder Julia held out to her. "Come on in. It's cold out there." Finny held the door for her, then closed it against the chilled air. She opened the file. "What the— Julia, this is the contract I gave you to type this afternoon." She glanced up from the pages. "I don't understand. Why are you bringing it now?"

"You said you needed it as soon as possible."

"You mean you've been working on it all evening? Julia, tomorrow would have been soon enough. I didn't mean for you to go to all this trouble."

The rosy color in Julia's cheeks deepened, and her gaze shifted to the floor. "I'm sorry," she murmured. "I thought it was terribly important."

Finny tried vainly to remember what she'd told Julia when she gave her the work to do. It was a simple contract, nothing urgent. What could she have said to make Julia think it so vital? She'd never shown such dedication before.

"Would you like a drink? It's the least I can do for ruining your evening."

Julia looked up with a relieved smile. "That would be nice."

"Let me take your coat."

In her white silk shirt and pale pink suit, Julia looked like an animated valentine. She fluffed her lacy collar and glanced around the room. "I've been dying to see your house. Elaine said you've worked real hard on it." Her eyes sidled over the entryway as Finny hung her coat on the hat tree beside the stairs.

"Yeah, I have, but I enjoy it. Come on in." She followed

Julia into the living room and motioned toward the sofa on her way to the tape deck. "Sit down." She turned down the volume and looked back over her shoulder at Julia. "Excuse the mess. I've been stripping paint."

"Oh." Julia's gaze moved over the fireplace, passing indifferently over the oaken flowers. "Don't you get tired of working on all this? I mean, don't you feel like you'll never get done?"

Finny shrugged. "Sometimes." She glanced at the debris piled in front of the fireplace, but her eyes were drawn back to the work she'd done that evening. She knew every centimeter of the wooden garden she'd liberated from paint. She smiled.

Julia's eyes stopped at the bottle of Amaretto and the glass beside it. "Would you like some?" Finny asked. "There's brandy and some Chablis if you'd like something else. Or some scotch."

"Amaretto would be nice. I hope I'm not interrupting anything. I'd feel just awful if you had a date over or something."

Finny gestured toward her jeans and T-shirt. "You can see I'm all ready for a wild evening."

Julia shifted on her perch at the edge of the sofa. "It's been such a busy day. Mr. Fulton was such a whirlwind, I could hardly keep up with him." Her lips curved in a fond smile. "He's really a dynamo, isn't he?"

Finny had gone into the adjoining dining room and was sliding a glass from the sideboard shelf. "I think the term is 'workaholic.' " She closed the leaded glass door.

"He wanted everything done by yesterday so that he could leave early."

Finny returned to the coffee table and poured a small

measure into the glass. "Here you are." She sat down at the other end of the sofa while Julia took a dainty sip of the liqueur.

"I just love Amaretto," she confided. "It always makes me feel so elegant."

Finny smiled thinly. "Yeah, me too."

Julia sipped again and put her glass on the table. Her dimpled, little-girl hands smoothed the folds of her skirt, and she arranged a smile on her face.

Finny forced her lips to reciprocate. She supposed Julia wasn't so different than she'd been when she first started out, and it should have forged some kind of bond, but Julia's Bambi-like demeanor made her want to smoke and drink and talk dirty.

"I really want to congratulate you on your presentation this morning. I heard it was very impressive."

"Thank you."

"I know that Mr. Fulton was very proud of you."

Finny was surprised she'd brought it up. The sharp look of embarrassment on Julia's face that morning when she walked in on Finny and Elliot in the conference room had been as effective an inhibitor as a bucket of icy water. She reached for her glass and filled it from the bottle on the table. Could it have been Julia who'd told Greg about that?

The click of the cassette player turning off was loud in the awkward silence.

"You know," Julia said softly, "I think this is the first time you and I have ever talked alone. At the office there's almost always somebody around. It's kind of funny. I've been wanting to talk to you for a long time." Her wide blue eyes met Finny's gaze, then quickly glanced away. "I'm really enjoying my job, you know, but I want to advance. You're sort of a role model for me."

"That's flattering," Finny said. Damn, but it was getting hard to talk.

"I've been hoping—I mean, it would be real helpful if maybe you could teach me—"

Julia's shy confusion struck her as overdone. How old was the girl? Twenty-five or -six? She was coming across like Dorothy without the glittery shoes. Maybe the Wicked Witch of the West had had a point.

"I doubt if I could be that useful to you before I go."

"Before you go?" An expression both mature and calculating flitted across Julia's face so quickly that Finny wasn't sure she'd seen it. "Go where?"

Home to Tara. "I'm quitting." Finny listened to the words, liking the sound of them. It was the first time she'd said them out loud.

"But I thought you—Elaine said that you were going to be promoted—did I get that wrong?"

"Elaine said that I'd advanced higher than any woman in the company and that the world was my oyster, right?" Finny laughed cynically. "Elaine likes to point me out as one of the pioneers."

Julia watched her with troubled eyes.

"I'm tired. I don't enjoy what I do anymore." Finny shrugged. "I figure that means it's time to shake the dice again."

"But, after all you've done . . ." Julia fluttered. "I can't imagine Lakin & Fulton without you."

"There are plenty there who can," Finny returned promptly. "Greg Hilliard being at the top of that particular list."

At the embarrassment on Julia's face, Finny felt a stab of self-contempt. What a savvy lady. Decided to cut loose from her job, got drunk and blabbed to the first person she saw.

Finny's breath gusted in a sigh. "I told you that I wouldn't be of much use to you. But you've learned one thing, I hope. Don't talk too much."

Julia looked down at her hands. "I—sure, I know what you mean. Uh, could I make you some coffee or something?"

Finny shook her head. "No, thanks, Julia." She got to her feet. "I appreciate your bringing the contract by. I'm sorry about your evening."

Julia put her half-empty glass on the table and stood up. "I was glad to do it." She followed Finny into the foyer and took her coat from the brass coat rack. "Thanks for the drink."

"You're welcome." Finny's head was pounding, and she was wishing she'd kept her mouth shut. "Can I ask you for a favor?"

"Yes?"

"Uh, that business about quitting . . ." Finny rubbed her thumb along the edge of the banister. "I haven't talked to anyone about any of this. I shouldn't have mentioned it. Would you keep it to yourself for a while?"

Julia's apprehension slid into a relieved smile. "Sure, I won't tell anybody. There isn't anybody who—" Her glance darted away from Finny's. "I won't tell anyone."

"I'd appreciate it," Finny said.

"Good night. And thanks again for the drink."

Finny closed the door behind her and leaned her forehead against the cool glass of the window. Loose lips sink ships, dummy.

She slid the bolt into the door plate. Julia had no reason to keep it to herself. The scenarios unwound with increasing speed: Julia confiding in her trustful way to one of the barracudas at the office. Maybe Greg, who would scatter the news around like confetti on New Year's Eve. Elliot's hearing of her plan to resign and calling her in to ask about it. That would be enough to send her back to Julia's level of development. He'd be hurt. After the way he acted today, who knew how he'd react to something like that?

Why hadn't she kept her mouth shut? She pushed away from the door and went to the kitchen. She should have taken her up on her offer to make that coffee. Except, knowing Julia, she probably would have made decaffeinated.

CHAPTER

2

A fine, sullen rain drifted down. The tires splashed over the pavement, shushing any sounds that hadn't been stilled by the wet night.

Elliot lived in the old Bonnie Brae area—not that far from Finny's Capitol Hill home—but a sense of journey crept over her, maybe because of the weather or the lack of traffic. She felt as though she'd been traveling for a long time.

Sheet lightning lit the sky as she passed the old Phipps mansion. "Add a light in the tower and a girl jogging in her nightie and we're all set," Finny muttered. The car's right front tire bounced in and out of a pothole.

She pulled up to a stoplight and waited to cross the street. A nearly empty bus roared through the intersection, its exhaust swallowed in the wet air.

God, but she didn't want to do this. It would be hard enough without the way Elliot had kissed her this morning, as if their long-dead affair had revived. Maybe that was why she felt it so urgent to talk to him tonight.

The line had been busy when she'd called him. All three times. The taunt of the busy signal became the sound of betrayal. Julia had seemed sincere. But she'd said she wanted to advance. How better to spotlight her own loyalty than to make sure Elliot heard of Finny's decision?

The light changed, and Finny's car splashed through a flooded storm drain. It didn't matter what Julia did. The point was that she had to tell Elliot about her resignation, and too much Amaretto had convinced her she ought to do it now. After the years of struggle, getting the MBA, working her way up in the company, she was going to throw it all away to work on old houses. She had to be the one to let Elliot know because he'd question the mental health of anyone else who brought him the news.

The windshield wipers struggled with the thickening rain. Finny turned on the defroster to clear the condensation on the window. It was a filthy night to be out. Elliot would be himself again, with none of the overtones she'd felt this morning. He'd probably laugh at her paranoia. How many times had he teased her out of her current crisis? "Just like a woman," he'd say, mimicking Colter's flat Oklahoma drawl. He'd always known how to read her.

The day he hired her he had seen through the assertive handshakes and deliberate eye contact with which she was trying to mask her inexperience. She was unnerved by the penetrating assessment in his pale eyes as he watched her from behind his desk. The knocking of her knees was registering on the Richter scale. Then Elliot smiled. His eyes, the same pale silver as his hair, warmed with humor and his deep voice was friendly.

13

"Welcome to the firm, Miss Aletter. I'm looking forward to working with you." She later learned that he had meant it. And it had become so much more than that.

Elliot always demanded her best. He had recognized her talent before she did and helped her transform her education into skill. He taught her that working with money was an intricate game, to be played with integrity. "You play tough, but clean." The challenge was to go beyond the numbers to the heart of the endeavor: it was a hunt.

"Haven't you ever wondered why we all talk of 'making a killing?'" Elliot asked her once, his eyes gleaming with amusement. "My God, look at the history of the stock market. As human activities go, it's on a par with stalking tigers with a spear."

Finny was damned good with a spear. She enjoyed competing and winning. It was only in the last year or so that the pleasure had drained away. There were only so many adrenaline highs allotted for climbing interest rates, and she'd used up hers. L&F had grown, and now the push was for the big institutional investors. Computerized, homogenized—her excitement had been amortized. There wasn't much room for the inspired guesses and winging-it hunches that had made the hunt so much fun. Even the options market had been tamed. No more spears.

The wet darkness in the rearview mirror was shattered by lights speeding up from behind. Before she could react, the lights burst into the flashing red and blue of an emergency vehicle. Finny swerved the car sharply to the curb. A police ambulance streaked past, swift and silent.

Finny's heartbeat thundered in her ears. Much closer and she'd have needed the ambulance herself. She took a deep breath and steered the car back into the street. "Let's get this over with," she said out loud. She was cold, and she needed a drink to warm her. However Elliot reacted to her news, he would give her a drink.

Finny saw the aura of throbbing color above the trees before she turned. The cluster of police cars in the circular drive signaled trouble, the ambulance disaster. It took an instant for the message to flash from eye to brain. Then her heart kicked into double time. Fear lodged in her guts. She floored the accelerator, and her Datsun snarled up to the police cars and braked. The ambulance lights shot holes into the dark and ricocheted from the neighbors' windows.

Finny slid out of her car and ran between two police cruisers. She collided with the plastic police line strung between stakes in front of the house, tripping over it as it dropped, falling to the ground. Her hands skidded against wet grass as she pushed herself to her feet. Her pulse was drumming in her ears as she sped to the house.

"You! Hey, stop!" a voice hailed from behind her. Finny ran faster toward the front steps. A hand clutched at her shoulder but she jerked herself out of the grasp and took the steps two at a time, hitting her arm on the frame as she charged through the open door.

She heard voices and ran toward them. Light poured from a doorway. Elliot's study. She rushed into the room. A flashbulb went off as she came through the door, and her eyes veered away toward the floor in defense.

Elliot lay on the rug. The blood that spilled from the wound in his throat had flowed down the front of his blue shirt. Two men bent over him, braced to lift him onto the stretcher at his side.

Finny's wordless cry was met with a frozen silence. She brushed by one ambulance attendant and dropped heavily to her knees beside Elliot's body. "No," she said, frantic. Her hands fluttered over his body, patting to stem the flow, to make him safe. "No. No." Her fingers recoiled at the plastic chill of his hand.

The tall man using the phone on Elliot's desk slammed down the receiver and strode to Finny's side. Straight, dark-brown hair tumbled over his wide forehead in a fringe at odds with his harsh features. Suspicious brown eyes looked down a long, straight nose that fit right in with the angular jaw under it.

"How'd she get in here?" he snapped.

The chunky, balding ambulance attendant rolled his eyes at his partner, who shrugged his sloping shoulders and shifted the toothpick in his mouth to one side.

"Lady—"

"Lieutenant Barelli?"

Barelli looked at the man who stood in the doorway. "Mendoza, what the fuck were you doing out there?"

The young cop's rubber rain gear dripped steadily onto the wood floor. He didn't wipe away the rivulets tracking down his face from the black curls on his forehead. "Sorry, Lieutenant. I tried to grab her, but she was moving pretty fast."

"Yeah. Probably does the mile in under four. Wake up, for Chrissake."

Mendoza's face turned a dull red. "Yes, sir." He escaped back into the hall.

The slight, intense cop at Elliot's desk glanced up from his swift search of the drawers and smiled to himself.

Barelli took hold of Finny's arm and hauled her to her feet. "Who are you?"

Finny couldn't look away from Elliot's body.

She looks as if she's been poleaxed, thought Barelli, and doesn't have the sense to fall down. She'd have pale skin anyway, considering the black hair, but that translucence came from shock. Christ, it was his night for hysterical women.

"Lady," he said coldly. Her deep red jacket was wet under his hand as he turned her toward him. "What are you doing here?"

Finny's gaze moved up the striped shirt, traveled blankly over the strong chin. He needed a shave. His eyes were cold and angry.

Barelli frowned down at her. *"Habla español?"*

The logjam broke. Finny cast a lightning glance around the familiar room. Five—six people were watching her. She turned her head away from their eyes, her gaze falling again to the corpse on the rug.

He'd held her this morning. Had swung her up in strong arms. Had laughed that deep, wicked chuckle.

"Oh, God," said Finny. She fought off the memory. If she let in any of it, any part of it, she would have to take it all in—the full flood of loss—and she couldn't.

Barelli watched her like a hunter. She was closing in on herself, shoulders hunched, body tensed. He'd seen it too many times before. If she got enough control, she wouldn't be of any use—if she knew anything.

"Come with me," he said.

"What—" Finny forced her voice through the lump in her throat. "What happened here?"

"Murder." Barelli glanced past her. "Eddie, we'll be in the kitchen. Keep trying Pete, will you? I need to talk to him."

17

The cop at Elliot's desk raised his head. "Yo."

Barelli took Finny's arm. "Come with me," he said. "We've got some ground to cover."

"Sit down." Barelli took a card from his suit coat pocket and put it in Finny's hand. "I'm Chris Barelli, Denver Police. What's your name?" He snagged two cups off a low cabinet shelf and filled them from the coffee maker on the counter.

"Finny Aletter." She sagged onto a chrome and wicker stool at the breakfast bar. The fluorescent fixture over the bar glared down on the white tile counter top. None of the other lights were on, leaving the white, modernistic kitchen in shadow.

"Here." He set a steaming cup in front of her and fished a small spiral notebook from the pocket of his tweed jacket. He led her through the litany of address and phone number. "What are you doing here?"

"I came to talk to Elliot." Finny's hand trembled so much as she reached for the cup that she drew it back into her lap.

Barelli noted the advance and retreat. Her fingers were rough, a couple of the short, blunt nails split and broken off. "Talk about what?"

Finny shook her head. "You said—murder in there. Are you sure?"

Barelli slid a pack of cigarettes out of his shirt pocket. "People rarely commit suicide by shooting themselves in the throat." He held a match to the cigarette and blew it out with the first breath of smoke. "Now, you show up out of the blue and I need to know why."

"I wanted to talk to Elliot and I—" Finny had a sharp image of herself punching in Elliot's number on her telephone again and again. "I couldn't reach him on the phone."

"What was your relationship?"

"I work—worked with him. I'm an account executive with Lakin & Fulton."

Barelli's eyes narrowed with surprise. "What did you do to your hands?"

Finny glanced down at them. "I was stripping wood."

"You interrupted that to come out here?"

"No. I'd finished for the night."

"So you decided to come out here."

The faint sarcasm in his voice was getting to her. "A woman from the office brought some papers by my house tonight and I—well, I told her I was going to quit my job."

Barelli drew on his cigarette.

"I hadn't told Elliot yet, about quitting, I mean." Finny's throat rippled in a swallow. "After she left, I started worrying that word might get back to Elliot, and I didn't want him to find out that way."

"Who was this woman?"

"Her name is Julia Simons. She's a secretary at L&F."

The telephone rang once.

Barelli tensed at the sound, then relaxed. "So you just came out here." He scraped the ash off the end of his cigarette against the edge of a white saucer that already held several cigarette butts.

"I told you I tried to call. The line was busy."

"Probably when his wife was calling us."

Finny felt as if she'd had the wind knocked out of her. "Marian. My God, where is she? Was she hurt?"

"No. Her son took her next door. She was upset."

19

The cop Eddie appeared in the kitchen doorway. "Chris, Pete's on the line. You want to take it in here?"

"No." Barelli stood up. "I'll be right back, Miss Aletter." She made no response. He walked to the doorway. "Stay here," he said to Eddie.

Finny's hands crept up her arms. She was cold. She put her hands to the mug of coffee in front of her and carried it to her mouth. At the first sip, her stomach rebelled. She swallowed against nausea, then put her arms on the counter and rested her head on them. Elliot was dead. The idea wouldn't fit in her mind.

"He can't be dead," she said aloud, her voice breaking.

"You all right, ma'am?" The voice came from behind her. She nodded against the corduroy ribbing of her sleeve. Don't think, she told herself. For now just breathe. She wouldn't think of Marian frantically calling the police while Elliot lay dying, his life gushing out through his throat.

The first sob came from deep inside and cleared the way for the rest.

Barelli stopped in the doorway. He raised one brow in question. Eddie shook his head and went back down the hallway. The red jacket Finny wore moved with her crying. It was the only source of color in the sterile room. He could barely hear the soft sounds she made.

He came up behind her. "Miss Aletter."

She made no sign that she heard him. He put his hand on her shoulder and shook it gently. "Miss Aletter."

"Leave me alone," she said against her arms.

"This isn't anybody's idea of fun. I need answers."

She lifted her face, blotchy from crying, from the protection of her arm. The anger in her eyes was blurred with tears.

Barelli put a small plastic bag on the counter in front of

her. Inside it was a small steel key. "You ever see this before?"

The key shone dully through the plastic. "No." Finny looked up into his watchful eyes. "Does it have something to do with Elliot's death?"

"Fulton had it in his hand."

"It looks like a key to a silverware chest," Finny said. "My mother has one like it."

"Do you know why anybody would want to kill Fulton?" Barelli asked.

"No, of course not."

"No enemies? Beloved by all?"

"I don't know of anybody who'd want to kill him!"

Barelli pulled a stool out from under the bar and sat down. "What time did this Julia Simons come by your house?"

Finny thought for a moment. "It was a little after eight."

"What about earlier?" Barelli asked. "Did you see anybody, talk to someone?"

"Wait a minute. Are you suggesting that I might be under suspicion?"

Barelli raised one brow. "At this point, everybody is under suspicion."

Finny nodded reluctantly. "I had a call from another person I work with, it must've been roughly between seven-thirty and eight."

"Name?"

She gave him the information about Greg Hilliard, wondering in some corner of her mind if Greg would admit to having called her. He was capable of denying it if he thought it would do him any good.

"You know," Barelli said, "I'm having a problem with part of what you've told me."

Her eyes met his squarely but he had the feeling that nothing more than willpower was keeping her going. "What do you mean?"

"Wasn't it kind of late to drive out here? After nine, and Fulton not knowing you were coming. Couldn't it have waited until tomorrow?"

Finny rubbed her forehead. "He was my friend. I didn't want him to hear about my intention to leave from anybody but me."

"How close was this Simons woman to him? Would she have had the chance to tell him?"

"Come on," Finny said. "You know how office gossip works. I was afraid Julia would say something and the whole damned place would hear about it before I had a chance to get near Elliot."

"Doesn't seem like much of a reason to drive over here," Barelli said softly. "Especially this late."

"I'd been drinking," she said wearily. "I got a little paranoid about what Julia might do." She glanced at Barelli. "It just seemed better to forget etiquette and talk to Elliot directly."

Barelli studied her for a moment. "Drink a lot, do you?"

Her eyes lifted to his, a spark of anger in them. "Not nearly as much as I plan to. I want to go home. Have you got your questions answered?"

"For now. Can you get home okay?"

"Yes. Can I see Marian?"

Barelli slid his notebook back into his coat pocket. "She was hysterical when she left here. You might want to wait." He stood up. "I gave you my card. If you think of anything that might have any bearing on this . . ."

"I'll contact you." She slid off the stool. "May I go now?"

"Yes."

He followed her out the door and down the hallway. She paused at the open door of the study, then went on toward the front door.

"Miss Aletter."

She stopped, turning toward him.

Barelli put his hands in his pants pockets and jingled the change in them. "Don't leave town without checking with me."

She nodded. She could feel him watching her as she walked down the hall.

The telephone in the study began to ring.

Finny let herself out the front door and closed it behind her. The rain had stopped, but the air was still heavy with moisture. She walked down the steps slowly, tired to the bone.

She became aware of voices in front of her and, as she came to the bottom step, she saw a bright light go on in the driveway. She got a quick impression of movement, and then another light flashed on. Television cameramen. She could see a channel number on one camera lit by the strobe light on the other camera. There was a van behind them, its signal dish tilted rakishly toward the sky.

"Hey!" shouted a man carrying a microphone. "Over here—Channel Seven!"

Finny veered away from the driveway and hurried across the yard. She heard more shouts behind her. The shadows cast by the strobe lights danced across the wet grass.

She ducked under the police line and ran toward her car, feeling in her pockets for her keys. She didn't know where her purse was. Had she left her keys in the car? She nearly ran into the uniformed officer who was standing near her car. He stepped aside as she passed and then put himself between her and the news people. They surged up to him like floodwater to a dam.

"Come on, let us talk to her," said one of the reporters. "You guys haven't played ball all night."

"Hey, Mendoza," called a photographer, "we'll get a shot of you, make you look good for your old lady."

Finny swung open her car door. She glanced behind her in time to see the cop's teeth flash in a smile as he stepped aside, letting the news people through. She slammed the door shut and locked it. Her keys hung from the ignition. She started the car and shifted it into gear.

The reporters swarmed around her car, strobes swaying drunkenly. A fist pounded against her window. As Finny eased the car forward, the headlights swept across the knots of people watching the house.

As she picked up speed, she heard an outraged voice. "Hey lady, don't you want to be on the morning news?"

INTERLUDE

*T*he concrete under the bridge was clammy as death and not half as friendly. A chill wind poked far enough under the supports to stir the funk of urine and unwashed bodies that wafted over the ragged bundles sleeping there.

The small man scuttling into the shadowed shelter didn't notice the odors and the curses that followed him as he tripped and stumbled over the sleeping or unconscious occupants, nearly dropping the box he clutched to his chest. He hurried to the southeast corner of the bridge, searching in the light that slanted down from the street lamp outside.

"Leila," he whispered sharply. "Leila, you there?"

"Shut the fuck up," a flat voice growled from the shadows.

"Over here." She had purchased further shelter from the night air with a cardboard box. He glimpsed her long white hair and bent to crawl in beside her. She shifted her shoulders so that they could lie face to face, pulled aside a thread-bare blanket, and waited for him to settle.

"I thought you might not come out," Bennie grunted as he eased down beside her.

"I wanted to see you. Where you been?" She swung the blanket up and over his shoulders. "I been worried."

The man wedged the box between them. "I got somethin' tonight, baby."

"You shitheads shut up!"

He lowered his voice into a whisper. "An old box, made of wood. Made good. And there's somethin' in it."

"Where'd you get it?" she breathed.

"South—past the Country Club."

"Lord, Bennie, it could be worth a lot." Her whisper grew louder in her excitement.

He put his hand over her mouth. "I don't want nobody to know." He slid his hand down until he could feel the rounded edges of the shallow box. "These bastards hear we got somethin', they'll steal it in nothin' flat."

She put her mouth up against his ear. "You didn't steal it, did you?" Fear crawled through her whisper.

"No."

She waited him out, and he added the rest in a breathy rush. "It was in a garbage can. Somebody come out and took a look at me but then he went away."

He could feel her eyes on him, even in the dark. "You swear?"

"I swear."

"He prob'ly wanted it."

"Too bad for him, Leila. I found it, plain and simple."

She pushed closer to him, pressing the box harder into his

chest. "What d'you think it'll bring?" Her breath was hot, and he could smell the musty, old-woman scent of her.

"Don't know. It's locked and I ain't gonna force it." His fingers traced the outline of the round lock. "If Larkspur ain't gone, he'll help me. He done some woodworking in his time."

They huddled closer together for warmth. The cold insinuated itself upward from their concrete bed.

A long bubbling cough split the night silence.

CHAPTER

3

3:07.

*F*inny shoved the clock back onto the nightstand. Her eyes were gritty and her mind had the peculiar unattached feeling that lack of sleep can bring. The sleave of care was raveling at a rapid clip, and it didn't look as though much knitting was going to get done by morning.

Every time she shut her eyes, she saw Elliot, dead. It was like a bad equation, one that her mind couldn't grasp. She had made love to Elliot, had touched him with affection and in passion. The fact that it had happened nearly ten years ago didn't make it any easier to accept that he was dead.

The stairs groaned softly as she moved down them, her deep red robe brushing against the brown runner. She snapped on the kitchen light and the room came to life: pale oak cabinets and muted orange walls; bright ceramic tiles glowing above slate counter tops. A floor of umber squares extended into a small, glassed-in breakfast nook.

The night peered in at Finny through the plants clustered on the glass shelves spanning the windows. She switched on the lamp suspended over the table to chase it away.

Tucked among the plants was her zoo of miniature animals: a bronze gazelle, the row of yellow china ducks she'd bought in London, a porcelain unicorn. She searched under the furry leaves of the velvet plant without thinking about it, retrieving a small donkey carved of pine, her thumb rubbing automatically against one drooping ear. Elliot had given it to her shortly before he ended their affair.

"Oh, God," said Finny and she wept.

Why had Elliot been killed? She'd asked the question a dozen times since she got home, and she didn't have any information to go on. Instead of finding out what she could from the cop, she'd fallen apart and come away empty. What about the key he showed her? Surely he would've told her if there'd been a burglary. The Fultons had more than enough valuables to make it feasible, and if Elliot walked in on somebody. . . . Or it could have been a random act committed by some crazy bastard caught up in blood lust. All you had to do was read the newspaper to know how often that happened these days.

She got herself a bottle of scotch from the dining-room sideboard and sat down at the kitchen table with it and a glass for company.

As bad as it was for her, it had to be a thousand times worse for his family. The cop had said Marian was hysterical, said it a little irritably, as though it were one of those unavoidable hassles of the job.

Finny raked one hand through her hair. Hysterical. A piddling little word to describe how Marian would feel, watching her husband of almost thirty years die like that.

How would their kids deal with it? Richard couldn't even stay in school long enough to get a degree. How the hell would he cope with murder? And Jennifer—

Finny poured some more scotch into her glass. Jennifer was probably the stronger of the two, despite having been spoiled from the day she was born. Maybe because of it. Elliot had seen himself as a hunter, but had staked himself out as prey for Jenn.

He'd been somebody else's prey as well. Finny's teeth clicked on the glass as she drank the rest of the scotch in a hurry.

She went back upstairs to bed and lay there, shifting around, trying to get comfortable, knowing she wouldn't be able to. Along with the horror was a sickening sense of relief. Now she would never have to tell Elliot she was quitting her job.

Sleep finally came, but it wasn't enough. She read an account of the murder in the *Denver Post* over a too-early breakfast of coffee, toast, and an egg she couldn't eat. She pushed aside the paper and thought of the day to come. Gossip, sliced and diced, was the only dish on the menu at L&F, and she, by virtue of having been at the Fulton house last night, would constitute today's blue plate special.

She dumped her mostly uneaten breakfast into the garbage disposal and wiped the counter distractedly. Every penny-ante rumor about her and Elliot that she'd buried with hard work over the last ten years would be disinterred before the day was out. If she hadn't already decided to leave L&F, today would have forced the move.

On her way downstairs from brushing her teeth, she knocked her red jacket off the banister where she'd draped it the night before. As she picked it up, a small white rectangle of cardboard fluttered out of the pocket.

The cop's card. Finny retrieved it off the floor. Detective Lieutenant Christopher V. Barelli, Investigative Division, Crimes Against Persons, Homicide Bureau. She rubbed the edge of the card with one thumb and felt the mixture of loss and frustration that had taken the place of the stunned disbelief of the night before. Crimes against persons.

Barelli had treated her with suspicion, had told her not to leave town, like it was all some grade-B movie. Finny snapped the card down onto the dry sink in the entryway. This wasn't a movie. He'd acted as though he actually thought she might have had something to do with Elliot's murder.

It wasn't until she was warming up her car that she remembered what Barelli had asked her the night before: if she knew anybody who might have wanted to kill Elliot. No robbery, no homicidal maniac—premeditated murder. As if you could tell.

She backed her car out of the garage into the alley. Elliot had made enemies over the years. He was too good at his job not to. If his murder had been planned and the police had to trace every cutthroat encounter he'd ever had to find his killer, it would be a long year. Elliot had played clean, but that didn't always make people feel better when they'd been skunked.

Finny waited at the street for a garbage truck to pass, staring at the yellow, smoke-belching monster without really seeing it. Elliot might have been killed by somebody she knew. A client maybe, or even someone at L&F. With the backbiting and intrigue that went on there, how crazy was it to suspect her co-workers?

Finny pulled out of the alley too fast, the Datsun's tires squealing. Elliot had taught her a lot of things, the foremost among them to get all the information she could and then to go with her guts. She couldn't bring him back, but she could use that particular spear to help the cops hunt down his killer.

She drove down Clarkson to Colfax out of habit: It was the safest street in Denver. As Denver's sex-and-sin center, Colfax Avenue had more cops per block than any other part of the city. The Colfax regulars, the hookers and bums, the pimps and johns, had turned in, but few of the straight-world day shift had come on duty yet. Kitty's, the main porn shop, still flashed its sign, cat-masked nudes promising erotic nirvana behind the grubby brick exterior.

Redemption was nearby, down a couple of blocks worth of small shops and Asian restaurants. The gothic spires of the Basilica of the Immaculate Conception pointed at the ragged gray clouds that scudded across the sky.

Finny drove past the dark granite capitol building, its gold dome shimmering. In front of the Capitol, two Civil War cannons aimed across the streets and greensward of the Civic Center at the Greek Revival City and County building. Rumor had it that during legislative sessions, the cannons were loaded.

She floored the accelerator and sped through a changing light. In a matter of minutes she was in the heart of Denver's financial district, parked under the upended glass and steel shoebox on Seventeenth Street that housed Lakin & Fulton, and was aboard the express elevator to the twenty-third floor.

Finny unlocked the doors to L&F Enterprises and turned

on the lights. She walked across thick, gray carpeting toward the reception desk. The offices had been redecorated last year to reflect the new colors and upscale look that Elliot's partner, Colter Lakin, felt were necessary to assure the clients of prosperity and wise management. Elliot had been half-hearted about the change, not convinced that mauve and gray and plastic had much to do with investor confidence. Colter had won that round.

Finny went past the empty desk, through the doorway that led to the offices.

Each of the account executives had an individual office, small cubicles for the most part, their doors lining the hall-way that opened into a large common area where the investment counselors and clerical support functioned. The desks were separated by oval partitions covered in gray fabric. Gray carpeting extended through the area and down the hallway into the private offices. The central portion had a soft, organic feeling, the gray upon gray serving to create a smooth, pillowed effect.

In her emerald silk shirt and camel skirt, Finny was as colorful as a butterfly in a winter forest. The brush-brush of her low pumps was the only sound.

She stopped in front of Elliot's office, closed now. Elliot liked the door open, liked keeping an eye on things. More times than not he'd been here early and had called to her on her way in to have coffee with him.

Finny made herself grasp the doorknob and turn it. The door squeaked a little as it opened.

The sun came through the room's one broad, bare window. Elliot's old oak rolltop desk was piled high with papers. His swivel chair was turned out from the desk as though he'd just stepped away from it.

Finny crossed to his desk and rested her hands on either side of the chair back. She closed her eyes, trying to imagine, just for a moment, that Elliot sat in the chair, that she could smell the Old Spice he favored, that she could hear him breathing. She wanted to remember him that way, not as she'd seen him last night.

It didn't work, and she had a panicky feeling that whoever killed Elliot had killed her memories, too.

Finny dropped into the chair and groaned at the chaos on top of it. Elliot had never believed in filing something if there was any available space on his desk. She found the Barchester notes she'd given him under a week-old front section of *The Christian Science Monitor*. His appointment calendar was partially obscured by an unfinished memo outlining changes in building parking regulations. One black leather glove lay across the memo. Finny gently pushed it aside.

He could have written something about yesterday, Finny thought, and drew the calendar toward her. A name, a place—something that might shed some light on his death. Yesterday's page, Thursday, had "Barchester" scrawled across it. A pencilled arrow pointed from the three o'clock notation to a single word printed in caps: FINN.

Finny frowned at the small page. Surely it couldn't refer to her. At three o'clock yesterday she'd been telephoning clients. Elliot hadn't asked to see her that afternoon, at three or any other time.

Earlier pages didn't reveal much. Clients' names were peppered throughout his work hours. A tiny star was written in the corner of Tuesday's page, another on the page for the previous Saturday. She turned the pages further back, but there was surprisingly little.

She pushed the calendar onto the desk surface and surveyed the stacks of papers glumly. She didn't know what she was looking for or even if it was here. It would take at least the whole morning to go through everything, not that she'd get the chance to do it, with no guarantee that anything there was relevant to Elliot's murder.

The office air pressure changed with the muffled thud that meant the front doors had been opened. Voices were coming toward Elliot's office; Finny stood up and put a little distance between herself and his chair. She creased her notes for the Barchester account and slid them into her briefcase.

"What are you doing with those papers?" The man who was glaring at her from the doorway tried hard to look like J.R. Ewing. And if J.R. had been five foot five and given to overeating, he would have made it. From the top of his wheat-colored stetson to the squared-off toes of his hand-stitched Tony Lamas, Colter Lakin looked as though he'd been successfully dodging cowpies all his life.

"I asked you what you're doin' with those papers, Finny." His drawl hadn't died before the man behind him eased swiftly into the room.

Greg Hilliard looked back and forth between the two of them with the alert opportunism that was as much a part of him as his guileless expression. His full mouth curved in a smile, but his eyes flickered as he gauged the tension in the room. "Well, good morning. You're here early."

"I came in to—"

"I want to see what you just put in your case," Colter demanded.

Finny bit back the hot words she wanted to say. "They're the notes I gave Elliot yesterday for the meeting with Barchester."

35

"So you just waltzed in here and took 'em?" Colter's round face was flushed with anger. "Hand 'em over right now. Didn't you hear about what happened last night?"

Finny fumbled in her briefcase, shaking with anger. She pulled the papers out and thrust them toward Colter.

"Miss Aletter?"

The man in the door spoke quietly, but he drew their attention immediately. There was nothing dramatic about his short, muscular body, and his blunt-featured face was disciplined, but Finny had the feeling that the externals were camouflage, and he kept most of himself hidden.

"Eddie Apodaca, Denver Police," he said. "We weren't introduced last night."

Finny frowned, trying to remember.

"Last night?" Colter fumed. "What'n the Sam Hill are you talkin' about?"

"I was at Elliot's house last night," Finny said.

"Lord," Greg said under his breath. "Are you out on bond, or what?"

"You mean you—you saw what happened?" Colter sputtered.

Apodaca glanced at him and he quieted. "Did you take those papers from Fulton's desk?" he asked Finny.

She nodded reluctantly. "Elliot asked for them yesterday, after the meeting. He was going to give them back today so I could finish my report."

Apodaca held out one hand to Colter. "I need to see those, please." He glanced over the papers, then folded them and slid them into his jacket pocket. "Did you touch anything else?"

Greg stood beside Elliot's desk, serious now, one long-fingered hand resting on the back of the swivel chair, his eyes grave.

"The appointment calendar," she told Apodaca. "I thought I might find a name, some indication of . . . something. I didn't disturb anything."

His glance at the desk was comprehensive. "When did you get here?"

"Not more than a half hour ago." She ignored Colter's snort of disbelief. "I woke up early, and I knew there'd be a lot to take care of today."

Colter stepped forward. "Fortunately, we have the kind of staff that can handle that, Sergeant." He turned toward Finny. "Give me your office key."

Finny hesitated, then pulled the key off her keyring and dropped it into Colter's pudgy hand.

"I'm callin' a staff meeting for nine-thirty," he said briskly. "Make some coffee for it."

Finny looked straight into his small, vindictive eyes. "Make it yourself."

CHAPTER

4

*T*he stock market could have crashed as soon as it opened trading, and no one at L&F would have noticed. News of Elliot's murder had the place buzzing like a convention of chain saws.

Some of the buzzing had to be about Finny. When, at the sight of Finny, Ardith MacKenzie cut off her sotto voce conversation with one of the other secretaries and jammed her tortoise-shell glasses back onto her ski-slope nose, Finny didn't think much about it. But at the sudden quiet that fell as she walked into the employee lounge, she knew they'd been talking about her. No doubt Greg had been playing Johnny Rumorseed again.

Finny's chin rose a little as she walked into the room.

Elliot Fulton's secretary, Linsay Tremaine, short despite her three-inch heels, was at the coffee maker. In her aqua shirtwaist, and still a little plump from the birth of her son six months before, she looked like a blonde pouter pigeon.

"They're saying you were at Elliot's house last night." She released the spigot handle and glanced up into Finny's face, her blue eyes red-rimmed. "Is it true?"

"Yes."

"I can't believe he's gone," Linsay said. "What happened out there?"

"I don't know. He was dead by the time I got to the house."

Linsay ran one index finger around the edge of her cup. "He was so up yesterday, really happy. He was so proud of the way you handled the Barchester deal." Linsay's glance fell back to her cup. "He had Julia and me trying to keep up with him all morning, and then he left early." Her voice broke.

"Did he say anything about where he was going or mention anybody's name?"

Linsay shook her head. "He just joked around the way he always does—did. Damn." She thumped her cup onto the counter beside her. "Why Elliot?"

The question of the day. Was Elliot's killer the only person who could answer it? "What time did he leave the office?"

"About two-thirty."

And the notation on his calendar had been for three o'clock.

"Do you know anything about somebody named Finn?"

"Why?" Linsay's brimming eyes met hers.

Finny couldn't afford to trust her. "I saw the name somewhere and wondered." She ripped a paper towel from the holder and dried her cup. "Is the name familiar?"

"No, I don't think so." Linsay started to move away, then turned back. Her round, pretty face had a determination in it that Finny had never seen. "You should know that there's a lot of talk about you today."

"There's always talk about somebody."

"Not in connection with the murder," Linsay said grimly. "Just watch out."

Linsay was right. Finny had expected some of the fallout. But by the time little Gloria Metzenbaum, whose mother had convinced her at an early age that rudeness of any kind was an affront to God and nature, had walked by her, pretending that Finny wasn't there, she knew that more than the usual gossip was afoot.

Colter wanted her out, not any more than she wanted out herself. But why were the gloves so dramatically off now? He'd been civil enough until today. Even if he'd been harboring the desire to get rid of her, she would have expected, if nothing else, that he'd want her to stay on until her clients were farmed out and she'd passed on as much as she could to her replacement. That had always been SOP at L&F.

Elliot hadn't said much about it, but she knew he'd planned to put her up for promotion. That was one of the reasons she hadn't wanted to tell him of her decision to resign. He and Colter had split on a lot of issues, and the power jockeys in the office had started lining up on one side or the other some time ago. Had it gotten so bad that Colter was willing to toss her out just to consolidate his position? You'd think just being the sole surviving partner would be enough to take care of that. Surely he couldn't believe that she'd actually had something to do with Elliot's death.

For the first time in L&F's history, no one was late to the staff meeting. Even Jon Darrow, nicknamed "Molasses" by his resentful peers in Promotion, trotted in seconds before the nine-thirty deadline. The plush, mauve cotton velvet chairs around the runway-sized onyx table cushioned the variously-sized, well-dressed behinds of the firm's management personnel and account execs. The lower echelons, secretarial and clerical support, presumably better able to deal with adversity by virtue of their inferiority, rested their nether regions on the stackable chairs of molded plastic, also mauve, that were arranged respectfully behind the others.

"Finny," Darrow called from three chairs down the table. "I heard about the Barchester deal last night. Good work." His broad, fleshy face beamed to the extent it was able, his eyes alight with all the warmth of a liquid display terminal.

Nonplussed, Finny essayed a tentative smile. Hadn't he heard about Elliot?

"Finny." Behind her, Elaine Leyden, head of clerical services, settled her ample body onto a plastic chair. "Is it true you were at Elliot's last night?"

Finny nodded over her shoulder, and Elaine shuddered dramatically. "God, it must've been horrible." Her double chin, camouflaged to the best of Elizabeth Arden's ability, wobbled sympathetically.

The hum of voices subsided as Colter Lakin strode into the room, Greg Hilliard close behind him. As Colter assumed his rightful position at the head of the table, Greg, studiously grave, pulled out the empty chair waiting for him in front of the latest receptionist, Lisa Parmeter.

Lisa squirmed in her seat, flipping her auburn hair over

one shoulder, demonstrating the flex in her blue jersey dress. She rested an unnecessarily compassionate hand on Greg's shoulder. At his murmured response, she bridled with restraint, as befitted the occasion.

"As you've probably heard," Colter said in simple sorrow, "Elliot Fulton was killed last night." At the choked gasp down the table, he paused, assessing the situation. Twenty-one pairs of eyes looked around at each other, trying to determine who had made the unexpected sound. Eddie Apodaca walked into the quiet room and took a seat near the door.

"Some of you have already talked with Sergeant Apodaca of the police department," Colter announced, waving a pudgy hand toward the seated figure. "The rest of you will be doin' the same thing before the end of the day." His well-fed face tightened earnestly. "I know that you will do everything you can to help the police find out who murdered Elliot. As members of the L&F family, you can do no less."

"Get me a barf bag," Elaine's voice whispered behind Finny. Out of the corner of her eyes, Finny saw Gloria Metzenbaum put her hand to her mouth.

Ardith MacKenzie—could anyone remember how long she'd been with the firm?—lifted her sharp nose out of the lacy handkerchief she held to it and glared at Elaine. There was a time when that glare would have outclassed a *Star Wars* raygun.

In an instant of understanding, Finny realized what Elliot's death would mean to L&F. "I knew that with Colter as my partner," Elliot had told her once, "I'd never be allowed to drift off into the sidelines. It's all just a balls-out plunge for the bucks for him. Together we have balls and brains."

Without Elliot to check his go-for-the-jugular style, Colter would update and streamline every bit of individuality out of the firm before anybody knew what was happening. The people like Ardith, who had terrorized her secretarial staff since the company's earliest beginnings, and Russell Byrnes, even better with older investors now that he'd turned sixty, would be pushed out. Colter had already played the attrition game with some of the old-timers. L&F would become a "fast-food" broker and the time-consuming customer service aspects would be as obsolete as a church key in a pull-tab world.

"—not close down the office since Elliot's funeral will be held on Sunday, barrin' complications from the authorities," Colter went on. "Elliot was a businessman, one of the best in this state, and he would not consider a day in which we are not thinkin' and doin' for our clients to be a fittin' tribute to his memory."

A disgruntled mutter hovered over the junior investment counselors and secretaries.

"I'll be lettin' you know the time and place of the services just as soon as I find out." His gaze moved around the room, skipping across Finny's contemptuous glare as if she weren't there. "That's all for now."

Colter walked out of the room as people pushed away from the table, and the low hum of voices grew in volume. Gloria Metzenbaum smiled timidly at Elaine.

"Where's Julia Simons?" Elaine asked Finny. "She and Gloria are usually closer together than Bonnie and Clyde."

"I don't know." Finny glanced around. "I haven't seen her today."

"Me neither." She slanted a look at Finny's face. "How're you doing?"

Finny eased herself past a clutch of secretaries and worked

43

her way to the door. "I guess I'll live." She glanced back at Elaine. "We can talk about it later, okay?"

She careened straight into a bulky gray suit. "Oh, sorry," she began, then broke off. The face Jon Darrow turned to her was pale, greased with a thin layer of sweat. His heavy-lidded eyes flashed in an instant of pain, then closed themselves off behind the flat stare he used on the world.

"Are you okay?" Finny asked.

Jon shook his head meaninglessly, his thick neck straining against the restraints of collar and tie, and shouldered his way through the junior account execs clotting the doorway.

Finny looked after him thoughtfully. She'd worked with Jon for ten years and hadn't ever seen him go beyond the cardboard joviality of tales about his exploits as a college football lineman. A man's man was what Elliot had called him, and, remembering the air of unhappiness his wife wore like a part of her wardrobe, Finny could only believe it.

"What 'his problem?" Elaine said.

"Beats me. He couldn't be that upset about Elliot; they weren't that close."

"He's not close to anybody unless he can buy or sell." Elaine's voice was bitter.

Finny turned to look at her. "What do you mean?" She brushed against Eddie Apodaca, silently watching people passing through the door. "Excuse me," Finny said.

Apodaca moved back a little and nodded impassively.

Greg Hilliard, freed from the bonds of hypocrisy at last and grinning like the grille on a '56 Buick, came up beside her and patted her shoulder. "What's the matter, Finny? Long arm of the law catch up with you at last?"

"Greg," Finny said calmly, "where did you get that disgusting spot on your tie?" and left him peering intently down at mild stripes of brown and beige.

By lunchtime Finny had reached her limit. She couldn't have been more shunned if she'd had a scarlet letter embroidered on her chest. Her fling with Elliot had occurred too long ago to warrant an "A." Maybe "PNG" for persona non grata would have been more appropriate.

The grapevine was obviously producing a potent brew. How much could she learn under these circumstances? Greg in his proto-Goebbels mode had made it impossible to discreetly pump any member of the staff. Even the people who liked her were giving her wide berth until things got more settled. What the hell had Greg been saying?

"—that you were there when Elliot was killed," Elaine said wrathfully a couple of hours later. "He doesn't come right out and say that you killed him," she snarled, "but he leaves it as a great big option for people to figure out for themselves."

Finny adjusted the blinds on her one window to let in as much light as possible. "Thank God this ain't Salem."

"Don't joke about it." Elaine was as definitive as a plump exclamation point in her black and white dress.

"On the contrary," Finny said absently, "I plan to sue the little son of a bitch." She glanced at Elaine over her shoulder. "You want to be a witness?"

"Finny," Elaine said seriously, "what are you going to do?"

"I don't know." Her gaze traveled around the office. Here, Colter's design scheme had translated into grays and blues, and the window was small. She'd added a Monet print and a large ficus next to the window, but neither had helped much.

"I've spent a lot of years in this room," Finny said. The best years of her life?

"And you'll spend a lot more."

Elaine was as loyal as she was efficient. Finny realized how much she would miss her. "Give me a break," she said brusquely, to mask the shake in her voice. "You know the skids have been greased as far as Colter's concerned."

"But why?" Elaine struck one arm of the chair with her fist. "He's in control now—why should he risk hurting the company by getting rid of you?"

"Beats me. I'm hardly in a position to lead a palace coup."

"I wonder." Elaine's carefully made-up face wrinkled in thought. "Do you have any notion of how the rights of survivorship are spelled out in the partnership papers?"

"No, I've never seen them." Finny rested one hip on the edge of her desk. "What are you getting at?"

"The usual setup allows for the surviving partner to buy out the other's heirs, at a fair market price, to avoid having them sweep in, trying to run the business. If you had real novices or wackos, it'd kill the golden goose."

"Sure, but I don't see your point."

"You know how much money Colter's thrown around in the last couple of years—all that 'new image' crap, and then that crypto-southern mansion of his out in Cherry Hills. He paid at least a million two for that. Is it likely that he's got enough bucks to buy out Marian Fulton, assuming that's who inherits?"

Finny stared at her. "You mean, if he couldn't buy her out, I'd be a threat to Colter?"

"Elliot's been grooming you for a VP for a long time," Elaine said. "It's reasonable to assume that if Marian inherits and gets involved with management of the firm, you'd be a primary player."

Finny shook her head, eyes narrowed. "It won't wash. Colter and Elliot were still friends, in spite of the Mickey Mouse stuff that's been going on around here. Why wouldn't Marian turn to Colter for advice and go along with whatever he tells her to do? She's no financial wizard. Besides, even if you're right, Colter wouldn't have anything to gain by pushing me out now. Marian could just bring me back if she wanted me to be her stand-in."

"Not if she thinks you had something to do with Elliot's death," Elaine said softly.

"What?"

"Greg's tarring you with a pretty big brush." Elaine picked absently at one arm of her chair with bright red nails. "That performance had to be for somebody's benefit, and Marian seems the logical choice, don't you think?"

"How the hell would she know?"

Elaine stared at her in amazement. "Which old bat around here has held the title of Chief Stool Pigeon since the Paleozoic Era, which was when she was hired?"

Finny closed her eyes tiredly. "Ardith MacKenzie."

"Very good."

"Jesus. And I thought Greg had a devious mind."

"It takes one to know one." Elaine's smile was modest as she moved toward the door.

"I think I'd better scare up a copy of the partnership agreement." The phone buzzed, and Finny picked up the receiver. She listened for a moment, then glanced across the room at Elaine. "I've got to take a call," she said wryly, "and you'll never guess who it is."

Elaine's eyes narrowed. "Marian?"

"Bingo. She wants me to take their checkbook out to the house. Elliot left it in his desk."

"You think that's the only reason?"

"Come on, you can't believe she could've heard anything already about the garbage that's been going on here."

Elaine stopped at the door, one hand on the knob. "Finny, you know the so-called grapevine around here is more like kudzu. The phones aren't dead, are they? Ardith probably called her right after the staff meeting."

CHAPTER

5

*F*inny sped east on Speer Boulevard, past the trees and weathered urns waiting open-mouthed for spring to come. She joined the rush of traffic past the Denver Country Club, mourning the lilac hedge that had been supplanted by institutional brick in the wall that now barricaded the club golf course from the bustle of the Cherry Creek shopping center.

She swung off Speer onto University and accelerated up the hill past the Calvary Temple, its wedge of purple and rose windows agrin at having survived another year of chinooks and blizzards.

Just another normal day in Denver. Blue skies, Friday traffic coagulating as commuters raced for a place in the Valley Highway jam session. No reason to get uptight. So how come her hands had a deathgrip on the steering wheel? If Elaine was right, and Greg's little song and dance was for Marian's benefit, what kind of reception could she expect?

She turned off onto Bonnie Brae and followed the winding street through the pocket of quiet elegance that slept between the college bustle of University Boulevard and the car-lot, fast-food flurry of Colorado Boulevard on the east. Here, manicured lawns studded with tamed and trimmed trees were the settings for dignified houses, genteely disbelieving that anything as untoward as murder could ever occur.

Finny swung the car around the cul-de-sac, scraping one white sidewall against the curb. The Fulton house looked as it always had, a two-story red brick Tudor, a suitable home for a successful man wishing to live surrounded by his peers.

The house's mullioned windows stared out on a spacious yard, carefully groomed even now, before the March winds had exhausted their supply of debris from less immaculate areas of town. The maples and honey locusts were sheared as severely as a batch of army recruits, waiting for new growth to clothe them.

The police lines were gone.

Finny rang the doorbell and moments later was enveloped in a perfumed hug. Jennifer Fulton pulled her into the house, her hand holding tightly to Finny's. "I'm glad you're here. It's been such a mess today." At twenty-two, in her jeans and lavender sweater, her short blonde hair pushed behind small ears, Jenn didn't look over fifteen. "Don't talk about it," she warned as Finny's eyes softened. "I can't stand it."

"Done any skiing lately?" Finny pushed the door shut behind her. "What the hell am I supposed to talk about?"

Jenn shrugged, her glance darting around the formal entryway. "I've cried all I'm going to today." Her eyes met Finny's, and there was desperation in them. "I mean it. Come back to the kitchen. I want you to meet someone."

She walked briskly past Elliot's study and the archway to the living room, her slight figure bouncy in the tight jeans. "Mother's in her greenhouse. She said she'd be out in a while." The redwood and glass conservatory Elliot had added to the house a few years ago as an anniversary present for Marian had transformed her from a putterer into an amateur horticulturist. It figured that she would take her grief to her plants.

Finny followed Jenn into the kitchen, stopping at the sight of the man sitting at the breakfast bar where she had talked with Barelli the night before. He rose to his feet, his square face creasing pleasantly into a smile.

"Bart, I'd like you to meet a friend of the family, Finny Aletter. Finny, this is Bart Cronin."

His hand was large, enveloping hers, the showy sapphire ring on his little finger pressing into her skin.

"It's a pleasure, Finny." Cronin's voice was mellow as maple syrup. He was a few inches taller than Finny and stocky in his yellow pullover and green slacks. Short sandy hair and keen gray eyes completed the Andy Hardy look. He could have sold snake oil or have been a scoutmaster. It was that kind of face.

"What was I—twelve, thirteen—when we first met?" Jenn was saying. "She's the reason my nickname's Jenn. Finny and Jenny?" she added drily in response to Bart's inquiring glance.

"Don't blame me," Finny said, as she had always said, "Mine came first." At the familiar words, Jenn's gaze met Finny's, then jerked away.

"I don't know about you two," Cronin said without missing a beat, "but I could use a drink."

"Yeah." Jenn moved toward the doorway. "I'll get something." She ducked out of the room without looking back.

"It's been rough on her," Cronin observed after a moment. "She's holding up pretty well." He picked up a pack of Players from the breakfast bar. "Want one?"

"No, thanks."

"You know, I'm perfectly respectable." Cronin lit his cigarette and exhaled on a sigh. "I've been vetted by Jenn's brother and mother, and I knew Elliot, although not well."

Finny couldn't hold back a smile. "What makes you think I believe any differently?"

Cronin narrowed his eyes against the smoke curling up from his cigarette. "Intuition. I feel vibrations."

Finny shrugged. "She's over twenty-one. I'm not family, and, as you say, you've passed hers. How did you know Elliot?"

"I'm a collector. He and I competed for a few things now and again."

"Who came out ahead?"

"Honors were about even most of the—" He broke off with a disbelieving smile at Jennifer as she wheeled in a cart of rattling liquor bottles. "You've got to be kidding," he said. "This is straight out of a thirties house party."

Jenn made a production out of hands on hips and the pout of disappointment, but her green eyes were bleary and her mascara smudged. "Doesn't anything impress you?"

"Only you, sweetheart." His lips brushed hers, and then he was searching among the bottles. "What's your pleasure, ladies? I'm a hell of a bartender."

"I'll just bet you are," said Richard Fulton. He strolled

into the kitchen, a blond-thatched preppie prince, from blue chamois shirt to khaki tuck-pleated slacks. L. L. Bean hadn't provided a matching demeanor—Richard was furious, his father's pale eyes burning in the young, angular face. "Don't let me interrupt."

"We're having a drink," Cronin said, relaxed, his intuition out on a coffee break. "What can I get you?"

"Don't you think your timing's just the least bit tacky?" Richard's hands made tight fists in his pants pockets. "I mean, the old man's barely cold yet."

"Richard!" Twin flags of color stained Jennifer's cheeks. "Stop it."

"Now wait a minute," Cronin began, "I think—"

"Back off." Richard didn't even bother to look at him. He lifted one hand to Jenn's face, trailing his long fingers along the side of her jaw. "As close as you supposedly were to dear old Dad, I didn't expect you to break out the booze the minute he turned up his toes."

Jenn's hand moved fast, hitting him across the mouth before he could jerk away. "Don't you say that, damn you." She was breathing fast, her face suffused with color. "You're drunk. Get out of here."

My God, thought Finny wildly. What the hell is going on here?

Richard pushed at the corner of his mouth, a thin, bright trickle of blood escaping from under his fingers. His eyes were hot with anger. "What's the matter, little sister? Did you still expect to have it all your own way?" As if suddenly aware of the room's shocked silence, he looked round, took in Finny at a glance, and choked out a laugh. "Well, well, if it isn't dear old Finny. Dad isn't in right now," he taunted softly. "Can I take a message?"

It occurred to Finny to wonder if he was drunk or crazy.

"Richard."

His head jerked toward the doorway.

Marian Fulton was barely over five feet tall and looked as substantial as a cloud of smoke, but her gaze clashed head-on with the angry pain in her son's face. "What happened doesn't give you the right to act like this," was all she said, but it loosened the tourniquet of tension in the room. Richard bowed his head once, then pushed past her out of the kitchen.

Jenn leaned trembling against the breakfast bar. "Mother, he scares me."

Marian swallowed. "It's been a hard time." She extended her hand to Finny and produced a smile. Her heart-shaped face had a curiously naked look to it, and Finny realized she wore no makeup. "Thanks for coming. I couldn't face going into the office."

"That's okay."

Marian was already turning to Bart Cronin. "I hope you'll try to understand," she said. "Richard and Elliot weren't . . ." She stopped, as if trying to think of the proper word. "It's been especially hard for Richard," she finally said.

Cronin nodded, eyes assessing Jennifer uncertainly. "Would you like to go for a drive or something?"

Jenn turned to her mother. "Of course," Marian answered. "You need to get out of here for a while."

"But you'll be all alone . . ."

"I'll talk to Finny and then get back to my plants." She pushed Jenn toward Cronin with a small hand. "Go on."

"I'll talk to you later," Jenn called back to Finny over her shoulder.

"Okay." Finny glanced back at Marian and braced herself.

54

If Greg's poison had gotten this far, she'd hear about it now.

Marian stood listening, her head at an angle, until she heard the front door slam. She turned to Finny, her face sagging out of its control, her bare-lashed eyes filling with tears. "Oh, God, Finny, what am I going to do?"

"And so, brothers and sisters, it does not avail us of the peace of the spirit to rebel against God's all-knowing wisdom and heavenly love. It is rather for us to bear witness to His love by turning away from bitterness and Satan's call for vengeance, which can only give rise to more evil. It is our task to succor the living, to reflect in our deeds our heavenly Father's love toward Elliot Fulton's wife, Marian, and his children, Richard and Jennifer."

The mortuary chapel was packed with people. Nearly everyone from the office had shown up, although, unaccountably, Greg Hilliard wasn't one of them. Family friends; competitors; at least one of the local SEC people, gray-suited and grave; Elliot's brother from L.A.; and the unidentifiables filled the pews that marched down either side of the plush red carpet that extended like a long tongue from the base of the elaborately carved pulpit.

The air was heavy with the scent of flowers and perfume and aftershave, with eau de damp wool and fur thrown in for good measure. Finny wanted to either sneeze or throw up. The portly little minister, whose lugubrious expression threatened to slide off his round face like an ill-fitting mask, was tipping the scale toward throwing up. Why did people who preached this way always pronounce it "Gawd"?

Finny blew her nose, a signal for the woman beside her, snug in the embrace of her mink, to smile in careful sympathy.

"Elliot Fulton's killer, by the grace of God, will be found out," intoned the minister. "And it will become our duty to forgive the poor sinner who succumbed to the pull of Satan. We cannot let the violence of this foul act blind us to the injunctions laid before us in the Holy Scripture, which clearly enjoins . . ."

Ask not for whom the bell tolls, thought Finny, it's probably a collect call. At the muffled sound of sandwiched bodies trying to shift position, she glanced behind her.

Greg Hilliard, hand in hand with Lisa Parmeter, stood next to the last pew, waiting while the people seated there played Noah's Ark and tried to make room for just two more. He assiduously avoided meeting anyone's eyes, but Lisa's glance flicked over the assemblage like a triumphant butterfly, the smugness of her smile guaranteed to spur speculation among the office cognoscenti.

"—to hymn number thirty-eight."

The assembled multitude surged to its feet, waited for the organ to complete its opening bars, then swept into "Amazing Grace."

As the notes swelled and rose to the chapel's modestly vaulted ceiling, Finny's gaze wandered over the congregation. Who among them might have wanted to kill Elliot?

In front of her, Colter Lakin was singing without irony about a wretch like him in a tune hazardous to the song's health. His parted gray hair was slicked down, the cowlick at the back of the part just beginning to rebel, like a seedling breaking through topsoil. Beside him his wife, Imogene, her ample proportions encased in black wool, sang along in a reedy soprano.

Colter would be easy to finger. For one thing, Finny hated his guts. But she didn't even need that. Colter and Elliot had been more at odds during the last couple of years than at any time she could remember, over the redecoration of the office, over hiring, over the whole question of image versus substance. Going by the iceberg theory, that, at any given time only the tip of anything major will be in view, Elliot and Colter may well have had disagreements that even the staff weren't aware of.

But it could have been anybody. Greg Hilliard was Colter's henchman and hadn't shown evidence of any scruples so far. Would he draw the line at murder? What about Lisa or Elliot's secretary, Linsay Tremaine?

If you went down that road, then even Elaine, standing next to Ardith MacKenzie, would come under scrutiny. Thanks to her jerk of a son, she'd had to pay gambling debts and, once, post bail to get him out of jail. Maybe she'd gotten desperate enough to steal, Elliot had caught her, and she'd panicked. Elliot had been holding that key . . .

Finny closed her eyes, ashamed. Anybody else doing that kind of thinking would focus on her. Elliot had never made any secret of his liking for her, and they had worked together a lot. No one, thank God, had ever tumbled to the affair, or she'd probably be in jail right now.

The hymn ended, and people sat again. The minister began the prayers.

Finny's glance skipped over the bowed heads to the bier. How ironic that Elliot's casket was blanketed with red and white carnations. Elliot wouldn't even wear a carnation in his lapel. He'd said they were the conformists of the flower world: little variety, no risks. The other flowers around the bier were fine: roses, baby's breath, glads, and daisies. But not the rest. The minister, even the songs they'd picked—none of it had anything to do with who Elliot had been.

The family pew was at the right of the pulpit, perpendicular to the rest of the pews. A filigree screen ostensibly separated the family from the other mourners, but whoever designed it had appreciated the entertainment value of watching the next of kin. The swirls of metal composing the screen were widely enough spaced so that those behind it could be clearly seen.

Marian might as well have been a statue. If she prayed at all, it was inside, her thin lips sealed shut, her eyes open, staring without blinking at the casket. Jennifer and Richard flanked her, each enduring the service: Richard with a fierce stranglehold on the rail in front of the pew, Jenn's small white handkerchief lifted from lap to eyes, a signal flag of distress. Cronin was beside her, his square face suitably somber.

". . . is not dead." The minister leaned over the pulpit, pointing toward the assembly like a chubby World War I Uncle Sam. "Who are we to weep when our brother Elliot Fulton is not dead? He lives!" One hand pounded against the pulpit. "He lives with the Father and the Son and the Holy Spirit."

Finny caught a slight movement from the family pew, saw Marian lean her head against her son's shoulder. The brim of her black felt hat was crushed against the side of her face. Finny fought back her own tears. She would not cry in this place.

". . . in peace. In the name of our Lord Jesus Christ.

Amen." The minister left the pulpit and went to the family pew. He extended his hands to Marian and her children and spoke in sonorous tones.

The gathering remained silent, then rustled into movement. People stood up, put on their coats, joined in the hum of conversation. The relief of the living flowed through the chapel.

Finny didn't move, letting the people down the row step over her. Her neighbor's mink brushed her face on the way out.

The man in front of Finny got slowly to his feet and groped behind him for his coat. She gaped at the ravaged profile he turned toward her. "Jon?"

Jon Darrow turned, finally seeing her as the flood of people got past her into the aisle. His eyes were red and wet from crying, his usually ruddy skin white and drawn.

"Finny, I didn't know you were back there." He seemed smaller, his beefy frame shrunken under the conservative suit he wore.

"Are you all right?"

He didn't answer. As Finny rose and picked up her coat, he came around the end of the pew. "Here, let me help you." He held up her coat by its shoulders and Finny slid her arms into the sleeves, grateful for the warmth.

"Thanks, Jon."

"Did you come by yourself?"

"Yeah." Finny fished her gloves from her coat pockets and smoothed them between her hands. "I'm not very good company today."

Darrow's broad lips twisted.

"I'd better go," Finny said. "Do you have a ride?"

"Elliot was a good friend," Darrow said heavily, his gaze on his shoes. "He hired me right out of college when he and Colter started the company."

What would she do if he started to cry?

He looked up into Finny's eyes. "I know how hard this must be for you. He told me about you and him."

Finny's heart jerked. "What do you mean?"

Darrow touched her arm lightly. "He loved you. Don't worry, I never told anybody."

Jesus, thought Finny. Who else knows? She took a deep breath. "Jon, if you were close enough for Elliot to tell you that, then he also told you that it all happened years ago. We haven't—"

Darrow went on as if she hadn't spoken. "I just wanted you to know that I understand."

"Excuse me, Miss Aletter."

Lieutenant Barelli had come up behind her in the aisle. He made a conventional appearance in a three-piece, charcoal gray suit, white shirt, and somber tie. He carried a topcoat over one arm, and his eyes watched her with cool interest.

"Yes?" How much had he heard? He wasn't reaching for the handcuffs yet, just sizing up Jon Darrow.

"This is my colleague . . ." She introduced the two and they nodded at each other.

"Jon Junior has a game this afternoon, so I'd better get home. My son plays basketball," he explained to Barelli. "Do you need a ride, Finny?"

"Thanks, but I—"

"I need to talk with you, Miss Aletter," interrupted Barelli. "I can drop you off somewhere if you like." The quiet maneuvering made Finny nervous.

"I have my car," she said. "Could we get coffee?"

"That'll be fine."

"I have to talk to Marian for a moment. It won't take long."

Barelli nodded. "I'll wait here."

"See you tomorrow, Finny." Darrow finished buttoning his trench coat. "We can talk then." He nodded in Barelli's direction and went down the center aisle.

Finny approached the knot of people near the pulpit. Colter Lakin had one arm around Marian's shoulders and was talking in a low voice. His wife, Imogene, was watching him like a guard with a prisoner, but her head was cocked to eavesdrop on the conversation behind her between Jennifer and Richard Fulton.

Red-faced and furious, Jennifer grabbed hold of Richard's sleeve, and he pulled his arm away fiercely. "I'll see you in hell first," he said quite clearly and was pushing his way through the people around them to escape through the door behind the altar.

"Wow, what's with him?" Elaine Leyden's pencilled eyebrows were raised high enough to become part of her hairline. She was chic in a long, dove gray suit, her salt and pepper hair tucked neatly under a floppy-brimmed hat. She took a closer look at Finny. "You look like hell."

"I hate funerals."

"Who can blame you?" Elaine lowered her voice. "This wasn't one of the better ones I've attended. Could you believe that preacher?"

Finny grimaced. "I guess his intentions were good."

"Then you know what road his feet are firmly planted on." Elaine sniffed. "Did you get a load of love's sweet dream?"

"What do you mean?"

"Greg and Lisa." Elaine smiled devilishly. "What do you suppose they were doing to make them so late?"

"Trivial Pursuit, what else?"

Elaine laughed, then pressed a gloved hand against her mouth guiltily. "I've got to run. Ardith hitched a ride, and I want to get her home."

"I'll see you tomorrow."

Colter was giving Marian a hearty kiss, Imogene looking on with the sour expression she'd tried to patent some years back. She latched onto Colter's arm as they left Marian, bestowing a smile of recognition on Linsay Tremaine as they passed her, turning it off as they brushed by Finny.

Marian was brittle with fatigue, dark circles as big as bruises under her eyes. "Are you coming to the cemetery?" she asked Finny.

Watch Elliot placed into a hole in the ground? "No, I can't."

Marian nodded. "We're having people over later this afternoon, about five-thirty. Please come."

"I'd like to."

"I'll see you later, then." Marian waited for the next person, the next condolences.

Barelli watched Finny walk up the aisle toward him. His eyes softened as he caught sight of the tears on her cheeks. Cool it, Barelli, he thought. You never could tell a goddamned thing about a woman by the way she looked.

"Here." He handed her his handkerchief. "You look like you need it." She mopped her cheeks and tried to settle down. "You want to sit a while?"

"No," Finny said. "I'd like to get out of here."

"After you."

His voice was dry, a little sarcastic, and Finny wondered if he'd overheard Jon Darrow or if he was just cold-blooded. "Why did you come here, Lieutenant?"

"I usually attend the funeral of the victims in the cases I'm working on." He glanced down at her. "You never know what you'll pick up by watching the mourners."

"And did you 'pick up' anything today?"

"Maybe."

They were nearly to the chapel door when Finny saw Julia Simons in the last pew. Her face was bone white except for the triangles of blusher stark on her cheeks. In her black dress and with her hair pulled back, she was obviously in mourning, older with it, little remaining of the girlish woman Finny had talked with Thursday night.

"Julia?"

There was no response until Finny touched her shoulder. She jerked away from Finny's hand. "He's dead," she said angrily. "Elliot's dead."

Finny withdrew her hand. "It's hard for all of us. I know you were fond of him."

"Fond of him." Her face crumpled like a baby's. "Yes. I was fond of him." She stood up abruptly. "I've got to go."

"Are you all right?" Finny asked. "Should you drive?"

"My ride's waiting." She pushed past Barelli and out the chapel door.

Barelli watched her go, eyelids at half mast. "I take it that she held Fulton in high esteem."

"Most people did."

"But not all," Barelli said absently. "Not by a long shot, if you'll forgive the pun."

Finny's hands clenched into fists. "None of this touches you, does it, Lieutenant?"

Barelli shrugged. "What do you want me to say? I didn't know Fulton."

"But he was murdered. And with the attitude you've got, whoever did it won't ever pay for it."

Barelli's smile was a social convention; his eyes were bleak. "I don't bleed for the victims, Miss Aletter. My job is to figure out who dispatched your friend Fulton. Shedding a few tears at the injustice doesn't come into it."

Finny wanted something, some kind of reaction from him. "So it's just a game to you, just a puzzle to solve."

Barelli frowned, then pushed her toward the door. "Don't pick at me, lady. Funerals make a person want to fight with somebody just to prove he's alive." He pushed the heavy door open and pulled Finny through it. "I'm not a good choice for it. I fight back."

CHAPTER

6

*T*he promise of spring had been in the morning rain, but the skies had reneged. What was left from Wyoming's latest storm was bearing down on Denver in roiling gray clouds.

"Hell, I forgot about the procession," Barelli said. "Where are you parked?"

"What?" Finny followed his gaze. One of the mortuary attendants was organizing the cars in the parking lot for the drive to the cemetery. His black coat flapped in the wind as he went from car to car to pass on instructions. The cars nosed each other, end to end, the smoke from their exhaust pipes dragged quickly away by the gusts of wind.

"Over in the corner," said Finny. "It's the yellow Datsun."

"We can take mine," Barelli said. "I'll bring you back here when we're done. Come on, it's over here."

She turned back once again to the mortuary behind her. It

was a one-story blond brick box, southern gothic with six fat white pillars lined up in front of it. It probably didn't matter where the final words were spoken; you were just as dead.

Barelli's car was a faded blue Pinto station wagon, well past its prime, filled with papers, fishing equipment, and what looked like piles of rags. Finny opened the door with effort and shoved a stack of papers toward the driver's side of the front seat before she climbed in. Barelli pushed the stack back toward her as he eased into the car.

"Sorry about the mess."

"It doesn't matter." Finny's eyes returned to the mortuary. She felt empty. It was over, Elliot was over.

She looked like *Ms.* magazine's idea of a professional woman, Barelli thought, armored in her little black suit. All he had to do was figure out if the tears in her eyes were for real or just self-protection.

Finny fastened the stained seat belt across her lap. "What did you want to talk to me about?"

The car chugged reluctantly into life and made its way toward the mortuary exit. "You worked for Fulton for nine or ten years, right?"

"Ten."

"I wanted to ask you about Fulton's wife and kids. You know, what kind of relationship they had." The Pinto's transmission squealed as he accelerated onto Alameda Avenue.

Finny had a vivid image of Richard Fulton as she'd seen him Friday, his pale blue eyes liquid with fury and drunkenness. "They get along fine."

"It didn't look like it back there."

It sure as hell didn't, Finny thought. "They're under a lot of stress."

"You said the night Fulton was killed that you and he were close."

"Yes," she said stiffly. "We were very good friends."

Barelli stopped at a traffic light. "How well do you know his family?"

"I've spent some holidays with them." Finny looked out the window at a group of children waiting to cross the street. One of the older girls—a big sister?—clutched the arm of a gap-toothed dynamo who pulled her into the crosswalk like a tugboat with an ocean liner. "I stayed with Jenn—their daughter Jennifer—a few times when the rest of the family was out of town. Stuff like that."

A horn honked behind the car, and Barelli glanced up at the green light. He drove through the intersection, braking once for the reluctant pickup in front of them. "What about Marian Fulton?"

"What about her?" Finny shifted uncomfortably on the seat. "What is this about, Lieutenant? What kind of information are you after?"

Barelli smiled, turning on the signal light. He eased the car to a stop, waiting against the flow of oncoming traffic to make a left turn. He pulled into a parking lot and put the Pinto between two parallel lines. "I like to get as much background information as I can about murder victims. It usually helps in figuring out who killed them."

"Now wait a minute," Finny began.

Barelli shoved his door open and got out of the car. Before Finny could force her way out of the rusted door on her side, Barelli had come around and jerked it open. "It sticks sometimes," he said. They made it to the entrance before the fitful rain began again.

The restaurant was open twenty-four hours a day and had

the plastic ambience associated with airplane travel. It was filled with families with small children and the kind of adults to whom the notion of families would be a foreign concept. The middle-aged hostess didn't bother to smile as she seated them in an orange vinyl booth.

Barelli lit a cigarette and slipped his lighter into his coat pocket. "You want anything to eat?"

"Just coffee." Finny slid her coat off her shoulders.

"So, you've been a regular friend of the Fulton family," Barelli said casually.

Finny's insides were beginning to clench like a big fist. "I guess you could say that."

The waitress was chunky in a uniform the same shade of orange as the booth. Support hose, one scarred with a hefty run, encased her sturdy legs, and she wore tired Nikes. She set an insulated carafe on the table and dealt cups to them with the smooth skill of a Vegas gambler. "You folks want some coffee?"

"Yeah," said Barelli, "just coffee." He watched the hot liquid pour into the thick cups, but his thoughts were on the woman across the table. "Did you get to be as close to Marian Fulton as you were to her husband?"

His voice had a sneer in it. Finny's eyes met his over the steaming cup of coffee. "You overheard Jon Darrow."

"You can't blame me for being interested, given the circumstances." He reached across the table for the aluminum cream pitcher. "How long were you and Fulton an item?"

"If you heard what Jon said, you presumably also heard what I said to him. It happened, and ended, a long time ago."

"I heard you trying to say that." Barelli stirred the ersatz cream into his coffee. "I also heard Darrow not buying it. Why would that be, I wonder?"

"How the hell should I know?" Finny met the spark of surprise in Barelli's eyes. "He—Jon Darrow—told me he knew about Elliot and me. Well, Jesus, that happened so long ago that I can't imagine him even being interested, let alone bringing it up at Elliot's funeral, for God's sake."

Barelli sipped at his coffee.

"You don't have to look so damned skeptical."

"You broke through a police line the other night, Miss Aletter. You unraveled all over the landscape when you found out that Fulton was dead. But as bad off as you were, you didn't say word one about any romantic involvement. You 'wanted to quit your job.' Today I find out a little bit about how much more complicated it might be. For all I know you two were shacking up 'til he bought the farm."

"Bullshit." Finny slapped the formica table top with an open hand. "What you overheard has absolutely nothing to do with Elliot's murder. You'd be better off in terms of clues"—she stressed the word strongly enough to make it an insult—"if you'd never known anything about it."

Barelli flicked ashes into a black plastic ashtray. "I'd be better off, Miss Aletter, if you'd tell me why you were at Fulton's house Thursday night. Didn't you take care of business that afternoon?"

"What do you mean?"

"What did you and Fulton talk about on Thursday?"

Finny shook her head, not understanding. "The Barchester deal. Elliot sat in on the final meeting."

"What about that afternoon?"

"What are you getting at?"

Barelli frowned impatiently. "Your appointment with Fulton Thursday afternoon. The one you forgot to mention."

"I didn't have an appointment with him. He left early to meet somebody."

"Somebody named Finny? No, don't say it," Barelli raised one hand as she opened her mouth. "It all ended years ago, right?"

Finny had the oddest sensation: like a spinning turntable, arm suspended over a record, waiting for the needle to descend. "Just tell me what you're talking about."

"Fulton had you down for an appointment at three o'clock."

"Huh-unh." Finny shook her head in a decisive gesture. "He had an appointment with someone named Finn, not me."

"I can show you the calendar page," Barelli said. "Your name is on it."

Damn it, what was going on? She'd seen the name: FINN, pencilled in block letters, a little crooked on the page. "It said Finn," she said flatly. "I saw it myself."

"When you were in Fulton's office Friday morning?"

The other cop, Finny thought. He'd told Barelli she was in Elliot's office, and now he thought she was in this up to her neck. "I saw the calendar. Hell, I did a double take when I saw the name Finn. You know ... maybe Elliot started to write my name and didn't finish."

"Sure."

Finny leaned toward him, elbows on the table, eyes intent. "I got to the office at a quarter to eight on Friday. The doors were locked, and there was nobody else around. And the name on the calendar was Finn."

It was irritating how he wanted to believe her. Barelli lit another cigarette. "Then how the hell did the 'Y' get there?"

"I can guess," Finny said grimly. "Colter Lakin came in while I was there and so did Greg Hilliard. Either one of them could've written it in."

"Got any guesses as to why?"

"Colter's trying to get rid of me. Dear Greg wouldn't need a reason—he's been out of flies for months."

"Flies?"

"To pull the wings off." Finny stared sightlessly at the flecked tabletop. "That must be it. Greg was standing beside the desk when I talked to Apodaca. He could've written in a Y and nobody would've noticed." She glanced up impatiently. "Nobody *did* notice."

Barelli's eyes held admiration. "Nothing like a conspiracy theory, is there?"

Finny curbed the desire to hit him. "Are you telling me that I'm a suspect, Lieutenant? Because, if I am, I want a lawyer here."

"It may come to that." Barelli shaved the ash off his cigarette against the side of the ashtray. "You're the one person who keeps showing up in this case."

"I gave you Julia Simons's telephone number to corroborate my story as far as Thursday night is concerned," Finny said. "Unless you think she's lying, I should be out of the picture as a possible suspect."

"You've been watching "Dragnet" reruns." Barelli crushed out his cigarette. "Yes, for what it's worth, Miss Simons 'corroborated' your version of events. You're a victim of linear thinking, Miss Aletter."

"What's that supposed to mean?"

Barelli was pouring coffee into his cup. "More?" At her

nod he filled her cup. "I'm not convinced you killed Elliot Fulton. But your involvement with him could provide a dandy little motive for someone else."

"Only if my involvement was recent," Finny said with impatience. "And it wasn't."

"What kind of marriage did he have?"

"First rate."

"Does his wife know that you and he got together?"

He could see the color rise in her cheeks. Her gaze dropped to the table. "No."

Her answer irritated him, and he couldn't figure out why. He didn't like it. "Is that a 'no, she didn't know,' or a 'no, I hope to God she didn't know'?"

The color in her cheeks deepened. "It's a 'no,' plain and simple. She's never known."

"How could you do that—get close to his family? No feelings of betrayal?"

How could she make him understand how it had been? "Sometimes you make a mistake, and instead of walking away from it, you stick around and pretend it never happened. Pretty soon, it's as though it really never did."

Finny took a deep breath and let it out. "Our affair was short and intense, but it didn't have a whole hell of a lot to do with what I needed from Elliot." She picked up her cup, warming her hands on the outside of the thick stoneware. "I needed a family, not a lover. Elliot felt so damned guilty about our—the affair—that he didn't seem to recognize how guilty I felt."

"So you both tripped out on guilt and went on from there?"

"Why can't you leave me alone? I just went to the funeral of one of my closest friends. Why can't you lay off?"

Barelli shook his head slowly. "Doesn't work that way. I'm the guy who's supposed to figure it all out. You have information I need. I can't leave you alone."

Finny looked up from the table, meeting Barelli's eyes squarely. "Look, I know you need information. I want you to find out who killed Elliot. But I don't know anything." Her hand clenched tightly. "At least not yet."

"Sure you do. You worked with the guy. You know his family. You know plenty. Were there any other women that Fulton had a relationship with?"

"No. What difference does it make?"

Barelli raised one brow. "Oh, come on. You're telling me you can't see what kind of motive that could be for Fulton's wife, knowing her husband is messing around on the side?"

Finny's eyes widened. "Marian? You're talking about a motive for Marian to have killed Elliot?"

"It's a reasonable angle to pursue."

"You're crazy."

Barelli smiled. "Am I? Do you know how many murders are committed by the victims' husbands or wives?"

"Spare me the statistics. There's no way that Marian could have killed Elliot." Finny thought of the grief she'd seen in Marian's eyes. "They were happy. They loved each other."

"Then just where did you come in? How much in love with his wife was Elliot Fulton when he was screwing around with you?"

"You go to hell!" Finny's voice thickened. "Elliot and I had something together. It wasn't just a—a sexual adventure. It meant a lot to me—to both of us—but there was no way it could last." There were tears on her cheeks again. "They had children, and a history together. There was too much that didn't deserve to be thrown away."

"You were both pretty noble, weren't you?" Barelli smiled unpleasantly. "You sure Mrs. Fulton never tried to spike your after-dinner drinks with arsenic?"

Finny thought of the crumpled defeat in Marian's face on Friday. "You leave Marian Fulton alone. She's been through enough. Just leave her out of it."

"Why?" Barelli demanded. "Because you feel guilty about stabbing her in the back?"

"Damn you." Finny stopped until she could control her voice. "The affair has nothing to do with this. It might as well never have happened."

"You're just a bosom buddy of the whole family. Jesus," Barelli said, shaking his head. "And my ex-wife thinks *I'm* nuts."

"You want to focus in on Marian," Finny flared. "Investigate all the little pieces of her life while the bastard who killed Elliot walks away."

"We'll be checking out other suspects as well, including you and anybody else he might have been screwing around with."

"But she'll know that she's under scrutiny. Can you imagine what that on top of everything else will do to her?"

Barelli lit another cigarette and exhaled a cloud of smoke. "There's something about this I don't follow."

Finny said nothing.

"The paramour defending the wronged wife. It doesn't fit the pattern."

"There is no pattern, Lieutenant, unless the maze that passes for your mind qualifies." Finny shifted impatiently in her seat. "Look, can't you understand? The thing between Elliot and me was a long time ago. It ended, we stayed friends, I got to know his wife. Well enough, I might add, that the idea of her killing Elliot is ludicrous."

Barelli shook his head. "Ludicrous." He looked across the table at Finny, a spark of humor lightening the darkness of his eyes. "Where I come from, with that setup there might've been a couple of murders." He smiled mockingly at the confusion on Finny's face. "I'm Italian. You poach on a woman's man and she finds out about it, you're dead meat."

"And the other way around?" Finny asked drily. "If the man goes out and poaches on some woman?"

"He sure as hell doesn't bring her home to meet the wife."

Finny looked away.

Barelli's smile died. "People have been killed for less, a lot less. I've got no reason to think that things couldn't be the same in this case. You know the bit about the thin line between love and hate. Being a cop has taught me that the line doesn't get any thinner than between husband and wife."

"My God, what's your problem? Elliot's murderer is running around loose, and all you can talk about is the deadly aspects of marriage. Wait a minute. You said something about your ex-wife." Her voice became strident. "What's the matter, did you get burned? Are you hung up on a bad divorce?"

Barelli's eyes darkened with anger. "That's none of your business."

"Did I hit a nerve? You're projecting your own hassles onto this situation, aren't you? All marriages have to be bad, and murder as a way out is so much easier than divorce. Why didn't you kill your wife, Lieutenant?" She was going to burst into tears in a minute, and she couldn't do a damn thing about it.

"That's enough." The ice in Barelli's voice could have frozen antifreeze. "Don't try to muddy the waters. Elliot Fulton is very dead. There was only one other person that we definitely know was in his house when he died: his wife. She said their son got home shortly after the shooting. Don't you think it would be irresponsible, to say the least, to refuse to consider her as a suspect?"

"Yes. But it's just as irresponsible to take the easy way out and focus only on her."

"That's not what I'm doing, Miss Aletter." He let out a long breath. "I'm looking for information. Can you think of anyone who might have wanted him dead? Someone at work. Think," he urged. "Someone with bad feelings about a promotion that didn't come through. Someone who might have had some reason to kill him."

Finny shook her head in frustration. "Do you think I haven't considered that? There was friction between Elliot and Colter, but—murder? I don't know. You've been asking me all kinds of questions," she added bitterly. "Didn't you question anybody else?"

"Lady, you have no idea. Do you want any more coffee?"

"What?" Finny looked down at her empty cup. "No, no more."

"Let's go, then. I need to get back to work."

Finny slid out of the booth. "I thought this was work."

"Close enough." He left a tip for the waitress while Finny put on her coat. She kept walking as he stopped to pay the check. He caught up with her outside. "You're welcome," he said as he came up behind her.

"For what?"

He reached out and grabbed her shoulder. She stopped walking, but didn't turn around. "For the coffee."

"I didn't enjoy it enough to thank you." She looked over her shoulder at him. "I think you're wrong, dead wrong."

Barelli's hand dropped to his side. "For what, exploring the obvious? You got something I can use, give it to me. I'm just fiddling around with what I've got."

Finny walked away from him. When she got to his car, she grabbed the door handle and pulled it. Barelli came up behind her, putting his hand beside hers. He tugged sharply, and the door creaked open. "Wait a minute," he said before she could get into the car. He bent down to reach for the papers in the front seat. "These can go in the back. It'll give you a little more room."

Finny got into the car and slammed the door shut.

Barelli walked around the car and quickly slid behind the wheel. He started the car and let it idle for a moment. "You know, Miss Aletter, there is one other thing I'd like to ask you about."

Finny's nerves tightened. "What's that?"

"Julia Simons. Where does she fit in all this?"

"Julia? What do you mean?"

Barelli put the car in gear and drove to the parking lot exit. "You saw her at the mortuary. She looked like hell. I just wondered why." He drove out into traffic.

"She worked closely with Elliot. I know she admired him a lot."

"How long has she worked at L&F?"

"I don't know exactly, a little over a year. She started in the secretarial pool, then filled in for Elliot's secretary while she was on maternity leave."

"So she's been Fulton's private secretary?"

"Essentially. She's worked with me as well. Since Linsay—that's Elliot's secretary—came back, Julia's sort of been floating. I know she wants to get out of the secretarial end."

"Hmmm."

Finny watched the windshield wipers. The rain was coming down more heavily.

"Do you like Miss Simons?" asked Barelli. "Or maybe I mean, does she like you?"

"Why do you ask?"

"The way she looked at you, I guess."

"I don't know what you mean. She was upset, but that's understandable, isn't it?"

"She looked like she hated your guts. She couldn't stand it when you touched her."

Finny felt a ripple of unease. "She was upset about Elliot. That's all."

Barelli shrugged.

"Dammit, she can't be a viable suspect. Remember, we share an alibi."

"What was she doing at your place?"

"When? The night Elliot was killed? I told you that."

"Tell me again."

Finny sighed irritably. "She brought some papers by. She thought I needed them that night, so she'd been working on them all evening. Didn't you ask her about all this?"

"Yes, and no one saw her at the office because she left before the cleaning lady came through."

"Oh, come on. You can't think that Julia could have killed Elliot. There was no time for her to kill him and then race over to my house."

"You don't live that far from Fulton's place."

"You're really reaching with that one."

The car pulled into the nearly empty mortuary parking lot.

Barelli drove to Finny's car and stopped. The rain was coming down in earnest now.

Barelli turned to her. She had to work to keep herself from flinching. Don't ask me any more questions, she thought. Let me out of here.

"Maybe I'm reaching," Barelli was saying, "maybe not. In spite of my biases, or maybe because of them, I'm a good cop. We'll find Fulton's murderer. Just don't get in the way."

Finny retrieved her bag off the floor and fumbled with the door handle. Barelli reached across her and pushed the door open.

Before she could close the door, he called to her and she leaned down to look into the car.

Barelli's smile mocked her. "You sure you don't want to thank me for the coffee?"

Finny slammed the door and walked swiftly to her car.

INTERLUDE

*T*hey sat like a sidewalk display, the seven men, their backs against the old red-brick wall of the rescue mission, with nothing between them and the passing world but the haze of booze they'd scrambled yesterday to get and guarded all night to keep. Dreams were hard to come by on Sunday: The liquor stores were closed.

The traffic on Twenty-third Street was clogged by the heavy trucks that carried dirt and rubble from a construction site nearby. In the cars and pickups that fumed behind the trucks, people viewed the drunks like marks at a carnival, their curiosity and revulsion tempered with half-remembered warnings and atavistic there-but-for-the-grace-of-Gods.

The man who rounded the corner of the rescue mission wore a long, olive wool topcoat, a ragged red muffler wound around his neck, trailing down after him—the Little Prince the serpent didn't save. His small, close-set eyes skipped over the row of men. Sparse, greasy hair was combed across his head like weft on a loom.

"Larkspur," he called, his voice high. "Hey, Larkspur."

A man raised his head, following the shrill sound to its source. His face was freckled and weathered by the sun, like a farmhand home from harvest. Tangled locks of gray hair snaked to his shoulders, restrained by a headband fashioned from a dirty scarf. His rheumy blue eyes, the whites yellowed like parchment, blinked at the little man scuttling toward him.

"It's me, Larkspur."

Larkspur rested his forehead against his bent knees, a stained backpack under his legs.

The smaller man knelt beside Larkspur. His pointed face quivered with excitement. "I gotta talk to ya, private."

"We can do that tomorrow, Bennie." Larkspur's hand trembled toward the bag-covered bottle at his side.

Bennie stretched out his hand to stop him, and Larkspur's long fingers tightened around the bottle. "Don't mess with me, Bennie." His voice was as cracked as the sidewalk he sat on. "I can't share with you today."

Bennie jerked his hand back. "I don't want no booze." He darted a nervous glance around him. "I gotta show you somethin'."

Larkspur shook his head back and forth with slow emphasis. "I'm no good to anyone." Easy tears brimmed in his eyes and crawled down through the wiry stubble on his face. "I've been living in hell too long to come back now."

Bennie leaned back on his heels. "Shit, Larkspur, you're all jacked up."

Larkspur cried, silent sobs and bubbling breaths. "I'm no good. No damned good."

"Hey, buddy."

Bennie turned. The wall-leaner closest to Larkspur was watching with a feral hunger. Head tilted back, eyes half closed, he smiled at Bennie. He'd lost his top front teeth, and his deep brown face gleamed with sweat. "You take his booze, I share with you."

"Fuck off." Bennie cast a worried look back at Larkspur. He was still curled over the bottle between his legs.

Bennie settled beside him to wait.

CHAPTER

7

Murder was a surprisingly rich source of philosophical speculation. Reality versus unreality, the survival of the soul. Finny sucked meditatively on a piece of ice from her wine spritzer and let her eyes drift across the people in the Fulton living room. Her gaze lit on Colter Lakin and Greg Hilliard, intent upon a just-between-us conversation. The nature of man.

Unfair. They were probably working out the best strategy to maximize Marian's investment income now that Elliot was dead. And Congress was going to vote itself a pay cut to help balance the budget.

Marian Fulton was still welcoming late arrivals, her outpost in the foyer shared by friends taking turns at reception duty. Passed to the living room for food and drink, theoretically overseen by Richard and Jennifer, neither of whom Finny had seen, the guests had unbent sufficiently to get past awkward remarks to settling into what their previous visits had meant: partying, this time with Colter as overseer.

The room had been designed for parties, two gray and salmon Laura Ashley chintz sofas the primary conversational grouping in front of the red brick fireplace, with paired forest-green wing chairs sharing small tables in the corners of the room. Gray walls and quiet landscapes, polished floors and muted area rugs all flowed together into a backdrop for slow kaleidoscopic swirls of social ritual. A fully stocked bar at the far end of the room from the fireplace served as anchor in the traffic pattern.

On the surface it was a party like many before it, despite the occasion, but tension roiled through the air like smoke from a damp wood fire. The chief condiment in this bubbling stew of discourse was murder, and the thought of it edged the laughter, weighted the pauses, and had the participants slanting sidelong glances at each other.

Julia Simons's glances were more pointed than others, Finny mused, watching her with Jon Darrow. Julia had focused in on Jon from the moment she arrived, cutting him out of the herd like a prime cow pony at branding time. She'd switched from her black dress to a gray skirt and pink cashmere sweater, but only her clothes were demure. The girlish cocoon was gone, and the hard-eyed, determined woman she'd become had pinned Jon in the quiet alcove behind the doorway to the living room with low, angry words. Jon looked like he'd just swallowed a significant dose of Ipecac.

Finny drifted closer to them, coming up beside Gloria Metzenbaum, who was hovering as near to Julia as she could get. For reasons known only to her, Gloria had chosen designer jeans and a tank top for the occasion, her thin, bare arms and sallow, scared-kid face making her look like she'd sneaked under the edge of the circus tent to see the show.

"Miss Aletter." She couldn't have been more dismayed if Finny'd come to arrest her. "I was just waiting for Julia and she—"

"Yes." She couldn't just stand here, obviously eavesdropping while Gloria watched. "Would you get me another drink?" Finny handed her glass over, waving her toward the bar.

"—just see what that does," Julia hissed from around the corner.

Jon Darrow was spluttering like a volcanic pool. "No way, you little—"

"Miss Aletter, what did you want?" Gloria held up the used highball glass. "I don't—"

"Sshh. Get me anything." Damn the girl. Finny leaned one shoulder against the wall, glancing around the room casually, but she couldn't hear anything over the laughter from the knot of people in the center of the room. Colter had returned to his intermittent role as unofficial host. He surveyed his audience, chuckling until he caught Finny's eyes on him.

"Then old Elliot just up and took the bet," he continued a little more loudly, turning one shoulder toward her. "Here we are, in business about three months and he goes off with a hair up his ass.

"Yeah, Elliot was a tough bastard. Smooth on the outside, but tough," Colter said. "Him and me didn't always agree, but we sure as sin stuck together on the big stuff. Like makin' money."

"Hell, Colter." The straw-haired man next to him chuckled, his prominent Adam's apple bobbing. "Nobody I know ever disagrees with that."

Jon Darrow erupted from around the corner. Eyes blank, the muscles in his cheeks bunched, he nearly collided with Finny as he strode through the door, Julia close behind him. Julia's face was flushed, and her eyes could have melted steel. When she saw Finny, the rhythm of her movements changed, as though the curtain had come down on a stage, the performance over.

"Here's your drink, Miss Aletter." Gloria Metzenbaum handed her a full glass, her wide eyes on Julia. "What's the matter?"

"Nothing." Julia glanced at Finny's glass, her mouth tightening. "Did Marian con you into helping out?"

Gloria gaped at her blankly. "No—oh, you mean—Miss Aletter asked me to get her a drink."

Julia made quick work of Finny's proximity to the alcove, suspicion spreading across her face like a stain on linen. "Hear anything interesting?"

Finny shrugged. "Colter's telling stories about him and Elliot in the old days. I needed a wall to prop me up."

"So you sent Gloria off for refreshments?" Julia's eyes dared Finny. "Don't patronize me."

Finny shifted the sweating highball glass to her other hand. If Julia wanted to join the big kids, so be it. "This is your day for taking people on. First Jon, now me. What's going on?"

"Just a party"—Julia turned the word into an obscenity—"to mark Elliot's passing. Drinks and good times for all." Her bravado wavered on the last word.

Melodrama had its place, thought Finny, but only if you

could figure out the plot. "What's your problem, Julia? I might be able to help if you'd just tell me—"

"Oh, yeah, you'd help me, wouldn't you? You're such hot shit—such a big-deal woman—" Her face crumpled, and her words trembled between rage and tears. "Think you can just use people—" As her voice rose, heads began to turn their way.

Gloria stepped toward her. "Julia, stop it, you're really blowing it. Stop." She grabbed hold of Julia's shoulders and gave them a little shake. Her glance back at Finny was apologetic. "She's really upset about Mr. Fulton. She doesn't mean it." She turned back to Julia nervously. "Come on, let's go."

She pushed Julia out of the room, and the listening quality of the room unwound. Finny frowned at the empty doorway in frustration. What the hell was that all about? She raised the glass Gloria had given her to her lips and drank, her mouth twisting as soon as the liquid crossed her tongue. Gin and Coke?

"Did Julia poison it?" Greg, a drink in each hand, paused beside her.

"No. She's still a little slow on the uptake." Finny looked him up and down. He'd layered a baby blue sweater over a crisp shirt that was nearly as white as his teeth. Solid gold studs peeped from the cuffs. The creases in his charcoal gray slacks were sharp enough to carve a turkey.

The smug cast to his face was begging to be wiped off. Finny glanced through the shifting bodies toward Lisa, who was homesteading the loveseat nearest the fireplace, where flames danced silently behind brass-framed glass doors. Finny smiled maliciously. "Everybody's been wondering why you and Lisa were late to the funeral. You're not usually that sloppy."

To her surprise, Greg's cheeks reddened. She'd always thought you had to be warm-blooded to blush.

"We had car trouble."

"Really? Run out of gas?"

Greg's smile congealed.

"By the way," Finny continued quietly, aware of the lowering voices around them. Any minute the room would fall silent. "If you don't stop your little whisper campaign about me, I'm going to sue your ass."

Shock stripped Greg's face of expression. "I don't know what you're—"

"You know." Finny had never wanted to hit somebody so much in her life. "I have witnesses who'll testify to what you've been saying, and don't kid yourself that I won't use them."

Greg made a fast recovery, his eyes narrowing dangerously. "Just try it, Finny. See what it gets you."

Finny held his gaze. "It'll get you more."

He waited one beat, as if proving he could, then sauntered off toward Lisa.

Finny let out an unsteady breath. Temper, temper. She'd just broken the cardinal law of office politics: Never confront anyone while backstabbing is still an option.

Her hand trembled as she brought the noxious drink to her mouth again. Maybe it wouldn't be a bad time to reconnoiter in the bathroom. Strictly as a strategic move, of course.

She came out of the bathroom a few minutes later and was nearly run down by Richard Fulton. He pushed her aside with both hands and strode down the hallway toward the kitchen.

Jennifer was leaning against the wall a few feet away. "I've got to talk to you," she said, her voice thick with tears.

"Jenn." Finny's arms went around her in a hug. The girl felt small, insubstantial under her hands, more like the child she used to be. The shadows under her eyes, the tired droop of her lips proved that childhood was a long way gone. "Sure. You want to go sit down?"

Jenn shook her head. "I don't want to go back." She put a trembling hand on Finny's arm. "I think you ought to leave."

Finny absorbed the tension in her stance and the glitter—could it be fear?—in her eyes. "What are you talking about?"

"It's Richard. He's been half crazy ever since Daddy was killed, and today he's worse. He's been drinking again."

"What does that have to do with me?"

Jenn pushed nervously at her hair. "He was so nasty to you on Friday. I just don't want him to say anything or hurt you."

"I'm a big girl. I thought I'd stick around and help your mom clean up after everybody leaves. She looks exhausted."

"I'll help her, and Bart's going to be around." Jenn fidgeted with the charm bracelet on her wrist. Finny recognized it with a pang. A sixteenth birthday present from Elliot, Finny had given her a couple of its charms. "I really think you'd better go."

"Jenn, I don't believe this. Do you really think Richard would harm me?"

"I don't know what I think!" Jenn shifted from side to side, the gathered skirt of her deep green dress rippling in agitation. "He's acting nuts, that's what I'm telling you. I don't think he'll—have a fit, or anything, but he looked at you so funny the other day and—" Her voice broke in a sob. "Oh, God, I don't know what's happening around here, it's all falling apart." She wiped at the tears sliding down her cheeks with the backs of her hands.

"Hey, take it easy." Finny put one arm around her and turned her toward the kitchen. "Let's go sit down a minute."

"Mom's in there." Finny could hardly understand her. "Don't let her see me."

"Okay." They were almost to the back stairs when Bart Cronin caught up with them.

"Where're you going?" His easy smile died when he caught sight of Jenn's face. "Baby, what's the matter?" He put his arms around her and cradled her against his chest. "Honey, it's okay."

Finny was aware of the growing noise from the living room. "Let's go outside for a minute. There's a place to sit."

"Okay, baby?"

Jenn nodded from the shelter of Cronin's arm and let herself be guided through the back door and out into the chill of the night.

Their footsteps were loud on the flagstone patio, ghostly in the growlights from Marian's greenhouse. The cool air curled around them in welcome.

The lawn chairs were lined up against the house wall, under the patio cover. "Come on, Jenn. Sit down."

She was still crying, in great chunks of sobs. Cronin sat beside her, both arms tight around her.

"What got her started?" he asked quietly.

"Richard."

"Mmmmm." He rubbed his chin absently over Jenn's hair. "He's been on a tear."

Jenn pulled away from him a little. "He scares me."

"He hasn't threatened you or anything?" Cronin's face grew hard.

"No, he just ... I can't describe it." Jenn took a deep breath and wiped at her face. She used the handkerchief Cronin handed her. "I'm really sorry. I didn't mean to lose it."

"Why shouldn't you?" Bart asked gently. "It's been a hell of a time for you, baby."

"Yeah, a hell of a time." She folded up his handkerchief and searched for the pocket in her skirt. "How about some scotch? You probably need it more than I do."

Cronin got to his feet. "I'll get some." He walked across the patio and went back into the house.

Jenn watched him. "He's probably glad to get away." Her voice was still husky from crying. "I put on quite a show."

"Oh, shut up," said Finny. "I'm glad you got some of it out of your system."

"It's just that I don't know what to do." Jenn shivered as a breeze swept across the patio.

Finny noticed the reflexive movement. "I'll go get you a coat."

"No, it's too much trouble."

"I'm cold, too. Will you be okay by yourself for a minute?"

Jennifer smiled up at Finny. "Of course, silly. I promise, no more fits. Anyway, Bart'll be back in a second."

"Okay, I'll be right back."

Finny went quickly into the house. She *was* cold. The heat inside was welcome. She went through the hallway swiftly, past the kitchen and the arched doorway to the living room. There were more people now. She caught a glimpse of Richard Fulton behind the bar, talking to a girl in a pink sweater.

Finny slowed momentarily. Surely Julia had left. The bodies between them shifted, and she couldn't see Richard or his companion for the crush.

It took her several minutes to find her coat among those jammed into the front closet, and she took another from the back for Jenn. If someone needed it, she'd have to hunt it down. She closed the closet door and started back.

Her footsteps slowed as she neared Elliot's study. The image of him, the way he lay on the oriental rug that night, flashed through her mind. Would she live long enough ever to erase that picture?

The door was open a little, and she paused. She could go inside and see the room the way it was before Elliot's murder. She had her hand on the door to push it open when she heard Marian's voice. "—bought it the day he died?"

"I think he did." It was Bart Cronin.

"Why didn't he tell me?" Marian sounded dazed. "He was always so excited when he added anything to his collection. He didn't tell me."

"That's not the point." Cronin was impatient. "Where is it now?"

"I don't know." Marian sounded farther away. Finny edged closer to the opening and strained to hear what she was saying. "—nothing on his desk when I found him."

"Maybe whoever killed him took it," Bart said grimly. "Maybe that's why he was killed."

"For a manuscript?" Marian's words were edged in horror.

"Not just 'a manuscript.' Do you have any idea how valuable—"

Voices were coming from behind her. Finny turned quickly. She walked toward the people coming down the hallway, smiling as she passed the two older women and the man walking between them.

Finny draped the coats over her arm and strode toward the back door. A manuscript. If Elliot bought something valuable, it might be the motive for his death.

She stopped at the door to the patio, her hand on the knob. It was the kind of motive that would exclude Marian from the list of suspects altogether. Her, too, for that matter. Barelli would have to recognize it. The killer would have to be someone who wanted the manuscript, who knew enough about it to recognize its value. Marian didn't know anything about Elliot's collection, and neither did she.

"Finny, are you going to open that door?"

She spun around. Cronin was behind her, three glasses grasped between the fingers of one hand, a bottle of scotch in the other.

"You scared me." She turned the knob and pulled the door open.

"What were you doing?" he asked as he went outside.

"Just thinking." She followed him out to the chairs.

Jennifer sat quietly, smoking a cigarette. "What took you so long?" she asked lightly. "I was beginning to think I'd scared both of you away."

"Never ask a gentleman what he's been doing," Cronin mocked. He set the three glasses onto the stone at his feet and unscrewed the lid of the bottle. "He might be forced to tell you the truth—think how awkward that could be." He picked up one glass and poured a generous amount into it. "Right, Finny?"

Finny watched him hand the glass to Jenn. "Right, Bart," she said thoughtfully.

CHAPTER

8

*T*he sun edged over the horizon, its beams creeping through the window blinds, breaking in narrow stripes across the bed. A bird had just waked up and wanted to tell everybody about it. Finny lay watching the bands of light brighten the cranberry red of her comforter into ruby. Her eyes were gritty and burning from lack of sleep.

The fragments of conversation she'd heard between Marian and Cronin had kept her awake and thinking most of the night. If it were true that Elliot bought a valuable manuscript just before he was killed, and it was taken, then it was pretty cut and dried as a motive for murder.

Cronin had sounded certain that Elliot had bought the manuscript. Could he have been present during the transaction? For that matter, what kind of transaction would it have been—an estate sale, an auction, what? It wasn't as if Denver were loaded down with the kinds of places where such business took place. Sotheby's hadn't yet come to town. Of course, all it would take was one person, a collector who had something to sell.

But Marian didn't know anything about a manuscript, and surely Elliot would have told her about it. Going by Cronin's comment, getting it was a triumph to be shared. Why hadn't he mentioned it?

Maybe he hadn't had the chance. Maybe he had meant to tell her and just plain didn't get to it before he was shot. The remaining question was the same either way: where was the manuscript?

What if Elliot hadn't brought it home? He could have bought it and put it somewhere else for safekeeping. The office vault, or a safety deposit box. But surely, by now, the police would have checked that sort of thing.

There was another possibility. The police could have found it and taken it as evidence. But of what? Given that scenario, the manuscript wouldn't have had anything to do with the murder. If it was in Elliot's study after his death, then it was unlikely to have been the cause of the attack. The manuscript was significant only by its absence.

If she could find out whether the police knew about it, that would be a start. She would have to talk to Barelli again. It was either that, or call Marian or Cronin. Great choice.

Finally she'd decided that doing something was better than doing nothing. She'd called the police department at ten-thirty—Barelli had been on duty the night of the murder, why not tonight?—but he wasn't there. She'd left a message for him to call her, knowing she wouldn't be able to sleep any time soon. At midnight she'd given up and gone to bed.

All for nothing. Despite her exhaustion, her mind had

performed like an overready recitalist, replaying the events of the last few days.

The images were indelible as night terrors: Elliot's body, every detail she'd refused to recognize at the time, preserved and displayed with merciless clarity. The raw, heavy odor that had hung in the study, and the falling-away feeling she'd had in her guts when she saw the police cars. Barelli's angry brown eyes and the urgency in Bart Cronin's voice. Jennifer crying.

Underlying all the images was a fear that she couldn't explain. Surely the worst had happened when Elliot was killed. What reason could there be for the knot of apprehension that had taken up permanent residence inside her?

Finny pulled the covers up over her head. She felt guilty and she didn't know why. Maybe what Barelli had said the day before was to blame. It hadn't seemed like a betrayal to her to become a friend of Elliot's family. My God, compared to some of the situations she'd seen during the seventies, it wasn't that big a deal. At least they'd remained friends.

Finny moved restlessly in her bed. She and Elliot hadn't been lovers for years, but the memory that filled her mind was of a weekend long ago, when Marian had taken the children to see her parents. Elliot stayed behind, ostensibly to catch up on a backlog of work. Instead he took Finny to a place outside of Estes Park, a small cottage beside the Thompson River.

It was two days of heaven. With the sliding glass door open, they could hear the introverted murmur of water over rocks. A scent of pine was borne into the cottage by the breeze easing down the mountainside. They barely slept, making love again and again.

That morning, after Elliot's wakeup call had reached its

logical conclusion, he held her tightly to him, his chest rising and falling as he regained his breath. "You are a love," he murmured. "Such a fascinating mixture of brains and bodyworks." He nibbled delicately on her earlobe. "The perfect woman."

Finny cupped his neck with one hand and gently pulled his head closer. She put her mouth on his and kissed him.

Elliot pulled back a little and looked into her eyes. "Oh, you are special," he whispered. He kissed her lightly and lay back on his pillow. "Special enough to share my greatest passion with."

Finny smiled at him lazily. "That wasn't it?"

The smile he returned was wicked. "Close," he said. "Very close." He rolled out of the bed and headed for the shower. "Get up. We'll have breakfast and then I'll show you what I mean."

In her mind she could still hear his laughter at her reaction to the tiny bookshop where he had shown her shelves of rare volumes. He'd laughed, but his beautifully shaped hands had handled the worn books with the same ardor that she had experienced. His eyes glowed as he pointed out the shop's few treasures.

"Books are witnesses," he said in a low, dreamy voice. "So many of the books—most of them—produced in any era are forgotten. Even some that were popular at the time." His face lit in a smile, and he picked up a faded green volume. "A few make a comeback of sorts."

Finny glanced at the author's name, Bulwer-Lytton, and shook her head.

"Oh, sweetheart." He spoke almost absently, his hand stroking her cheek lightly. "There's so much more to life than stocks and options." He slid the book back onto the shelf. "Finding a first edition that's in good condition makes me feel as though I'm holding a piece of the past in my hands. When the ideas in it give me something I didn't have before, then it's like talking to the dead."

She'd felt stupid and jealous at being on the outside of something so important to him. They didn't stay at the shop long.

Their physical involvement ended a few weeks later. He talked of loyalty to Marian and the children and how he and Finny had been cheated by timing. She figured the feelings of loss were the price she had to pay.

Maybe Barelli was right. If Elliot was so loyal to Marian, why had he initiated the affair, because he had, first with so-called business lunches at small restaurants, then asking her to work late with him. There was the seemingly casual touching: the one-armed hugs of encouragement and the quick, light brushing of her cheek with his fingers. Then the first kiss in his office the morning they both arrived before everyone else. He hadn't been casual about that.

Hindsight, nudged firmly by Barelli, told her it was shoddy. She'd been a dumb kid and had fallen for the proverbial older man. Then she was in love, with all the Grand Hotel excess of emotions that everybody went through, including the storm of tears when Elliot ended it.

"I'm a bastard either way I jump," he'd said that last night, "and I don't want to hurt you. But Richard and Jennifer need both parents. Whatever I can salvage is for them."

He held her while she cried. "I need you, Finny, and what we have together, but I can't turn my back on them. I'm not that much of a bastard. At least we can still work together."

It sounded so contrived now. Contrived and tawdry. He was dead; it didn't matter any more. She had believed him at the time. Now she had to ask why. Was it just expediency? She had kept her job and accepted their invitations to their house, pushing the affair out of her mind.

What should she have done? Walked away from her job and the kind of warmth she hadn't had since she'd left home? She had needed that kind of friendship, and it didn't hurt anybody. It wasn't as if she was taking anything away from anyone. The sexual involvement had been a digression of sorts and was quickly forgotten. If the sex was gone, so were the awkwardness and sense of conspiracy.

She rubbed her hands over her face. Her nerve endings were sensitized, as though exposed to the elements. At a sound from outside, a clinking of glass and metal, Finny got out of bed and went to the window, lifting a slat on the blind to peer down into the yard.

In the alley on the other side of the fence, an old woman was rifling through the garbage cans, droning in a low voice. Finny had seen her more than once. Her long white hair hung over a shapeless brown coat that opened over a gray print dress. Her flaccid face was nearly as white as her hair.

The old woman moved with graceful efficiency as she judged each find, carefully separating aluminum from glass in the shopping cart at her side. She pulled a ragged sweater from one garbage can and inspected it inside and out, as careful as a bargain hunter at a department store, muttering ceaselessly.

What little Finny could hear made no sense. There were many "he saids" and "and then I told hims." Throughout, her expression didn't change. No happiness at a good find or disappointment at a meager cull marred the bloodless face.

The ragpicker moved from can to can, continuing down

the alley, shifting slowly from side to side on swollen legs, pushing the shopping cart in front of her, stopping to pick up other people's leavings.

Finny's throat ached. She didn't know why she wanted to cry. The tears came fast and hard. She let the blind drop against the window sash and went back to her bed. Groping her way to the tissue box on the bedside table, she sank to her knees and let her head rest on the bed.

She cried for a long time, until the sobs were dry and retching and her head pounded. She crawled up onto the bed, her face pressed against the sheet, every thought emptied out of her brain. Her rough breathing calmed in the silent room, and she eased into sleep.

The shrill ring of the phone ripped through the stillness of the room. Finny's head jerked up from the bed, and she reached quickly for the receiver, knocking it to the floor. She retrieved it and answered.

"Miss Aletter? Barelli here."

"Barelli?"

"You remember, the friendly neighborhood cop."

"Yes, of course. I—uh, what time is it?"

"It's nine after seven." His voice was rough with weariness. "I've been out on a case all night. I thought your call might be important. I figured a working woman like you would probably be up by now."

The sarcasm went right by her. "I'm up."

Barelli was silent for a moment. "Are you all right?"

"Yeah, I guess so." It felt strangely intimate to have his voice next to her ear. "I'm tired."

"What d'you know, something in common at last."

Finny couldn't suppress a yawn. "What d'you mean?"

"I'm tired, too. Why did you call last night?"

The underlying impatience in his voice destroyed the illusion of intimacy. "I wanted to ask you—"

"Just a minute." He put her on hold.

Finny lay back onto her pillow, the receiver against her ear. The empty sound of the phone line was a change. So many places, incuding L&F, played Muzak for hapless callers left hanging. Of course, what kind of music would you play for a police department? "Jailhouse Rock"? "Workin' on a Chain Gang"? "Please Release Me"?

Where the hell was he? She could hang up, but then she wouldn't know any more than when she started, and that was getting her nowhere.

The thought dropped into her mind with no provocation. What if the police didn't know anything about the manuscript? If, for some reason, like the fact that she'd buried her husband yesterday and hosted his wake, Marian hadn't called them about it, then Finny would be giving them new information. Barelli was already suspicious of Marian. What if he figured Marian might have killed Elliot for the manuscript? It would be his speed. No, she had to be sure that Marian told them first. Dammit, why hadn't she thought it through? What the hell could she tell—

"Miss Aletter? Sorry to keep you hanging. Where were we?"

Finny's hand jerked on the receiver. "What? Oh, uh, I was telling you why I called last night."

Barelli waited a few seconds. "Okay, so tell me."

"Um." What could she say? "Uh, I was pretty rude to you yesterday and I wanted to apologize. I know you were just doing your job."

Barelli was silent for a moment. "And this occurred to you at ten-thirty last night?"

Finny gritted her teeth. "Yeah."

"Why don't I believe you? Why do I think that sounds like so much horse manure?"

"Possibly because you wouldn't recognize an apology if it sat on your face!"

"Ah," Barelli said smoothly, "that's better. Now, why did you call?"

Finny said nothing.

"Let me guess. You're hot for my body, right? You wanted to see me again, but you didn't know how to initiate the contact. Being a take-charge lady, you decided on a fairly common ploy. You'd call me and apologize for some slighting remark, and I'd pick up the ball and run with it."

"Look," Finny said dangerously, "you may be a cop, but that doesn't—"

"And when I wasn't quick on the uptake, you turned on me, calling me names so that you can call and apologize again some other time."

"Stop it, goddammit!"

Barelli's voice hardened. "That's supposed to be my line. Why don't you tell me why you called."

"How can you get away with the smartass routine?" Finny asked in spite of herself. "Aren't you afraid of getting into trouble for acting like that?"

Barelli's voice lowered in soft precision. "You know something, Miss Aletter? No, screw that, I'll call you Finny. I don't care about trouble, Finny, because I'm what's known as a short-timer. In exactly twenty-seven days I will retire from the force. Until then, I have to deal with the public, but, because the bureaucracy grinds slowly, when it grinds at all, I can be as goddamned rude as I choose, and as long as I don't step on anybody's goddamned rights, no one around here gives a shit about it."

He must think she was a mental case. "Retiring? You don't look a day over fifty-five."

"I'm leaving with twenty," Barelli said in quick irritation. "I started when I was twenty-three."

"Job too tough for you?"

"Look, lady, I spent a good portion of last night out in Globeville trying to figure out why somebody bashed in the head of a little nineteen-year-old waitress. Yeah, today the job is too tough for me."

Finny started to say something, but Barelli slammed down the receiver.

She hung up the phone, half sorry, half mad. He came on too strong, and then, just when she thought she'd figured out the game, he shoved the knife between her ribs.

She didn't know any more than when she'd started. She picked up the receiver again and punched in four numbers. "Give me the number of the Marriott Hotel." One down, two to go. She punched in the number given her by Directory Assistance.

The hotel desk rang Cronin's room. When he answered, his voice was rushed.

"Finny Aletter," she said quickly. "I need to talk to you about—"

"I'm late for a breakfast meeting. Can I meet you this afternoon, about two-thirty?"

"Sure, I—"

"Great. Come down here and we'll have a drink." He hung up.

Finny replaced the receiver and lay back onto her pillow.

First some information, then she'd figure out what to do next.

Finny was beating against someone's back with a small tree branch. It was a man, tall and thin, and his shoulders were hunched over the package he held to his chest. Finny's arm was heavy and tired, but she knew that she had to keep on lifting and bringing down the branch for as long as she could.

Then the branch went limp and hung from her hand. The man was turning around. He had Elliot's face. Elliot was dead, but he was turning slowly around, his eyes widened in terror, staring at something behind her. She knew that if she turned around she would see whatever was back there. She didn't know anything else except that she didn't want to see what was back there.

Then the cold that had grown from a spot between her shoulders began to spread through her body, and she was no longer able to turn around. The thing behind her was coming closer and she couldn't move.

"No!" Finny surged upward out of sleep. "No!" She fought to sit up. The covers were wrapped around her legs and she tore at them to free herself, untwisting the sheet, throwing it to the floor. She sat on the edge of the bed, her heart pounding rapidly. "My God." Her hands shook as she ran them over her face.

Finny went into the bathroom and turned on the light, her eyes avoiding the mirror over the sink. She closed the bathroom door and locked it.

By the time she finished her shower, Finny was able to face her reflection in the mirror without her eyes straying to some point behind her.

The raucous call of the telephone intruded into the bathroom. Finny ran to pick up the receiver so that she wouldn't have to hear it ring again.

"Finny? It's Elaine."

"Elaine." Finny's glance went to the clock. It was five after ten. She should have called the office.

"Listen, I hated to call you, but Greg has a question about the Appinger account. I figured you might need some time after yesterday, so I put him off as long as I could, but he's beginning to hassle me, so—"

"God, I'm sorry, Elaine. I was supposed to meet with Colter an hour ago. Have you seen him?"

"He was in early, but he left for a meeting, I think."

Finny shivered and pulled the towel more tightly around her. "What about Greg?"

"He wants dates for the most current transactions. That's all. I told him to check your log, but he said you might be offended."

"When has that ever stopped him? Besides, why would he bug you about it?"

"Because I'm in your office. Colter's been charging around all morning, and it's impossible to get anything done."

"Tell Greg he can use my log." Finny closed her eyes and rubbed the back of her neck. "Tell him I swore before a notary that it was okay. I'll be so glad to be rid of that cretin."

"What do you mean? Is he getting the axe?"

Finny groaned silently. She wasn't ready to tell Elaine about her decision to quit. "Don't get excited. I just meant that—hell, I don't know what I meant."

"You sound a little ragged." Elaine's voice softened. "How're you doing?"

Finny had never been sure that Elaine hadn't figured out a little about her relationship with Elliot. "I'll survive, I guess. I sure feel like hell, though."

"Who doesn't?" Elaine asked sadly. "It won't be the same without Elliot."

"Yeah." They were both silent for a moment, until the quiet hum over the phone line dwindled into awkwardness.

"I guess I'll come in a little while."

"There's not much going on. Colter's not due back until this afternoon. If you wanted to, you could— What?" Another voice could be heard in the background. "Just a minute, Finny."

"Sorry," Elaine said after a brief pause. "Gloria's driving me crazy today. She's been bent out of shape all morning because Julia hasn't come in."

"Did she call in sick?"

"No. That's what's bugging Gloria, I guess. But you know her, she never hits anything head on. Now she's asking what to do about Elliot's Rolodex. As if I'd know."

"Elliot's Rolodex." He had every number he used more than once in that thing. How many times had she seen him scrawl a new listing on a piece of scratch paper and stick it into the file? The typists went crazy trying to keep track of them. Booksellers, auction houses—maybe even the mysterious Finn—would be on it.

"I thought the cops took all of Elliot's papers Friday."

"They did. But Gloria was updating the Rolodex. I guess nobody thought to give it to them. I sure didn't."

"I'd like to see it."

"Gloria was going to give it back to Linsay this morning."

"Can you get hold of it? There might be something in it that would help clear up his death."

"So let's give it to the cops."

"Eventually," Finny said. "Elliot bought something the day he died, and it would help Marian a lot if she knew who the seller was. If I can find it for her . . ."

"Finny, what about the cops?"

"I won't keep it for long. I just want to see it."

"Okay, but the sooner the better."

"I'll be there in a jiffy."

"If you want, I can bring it over. It'd be great to get out of here."

"I told Colter I'd talk to him."

"Terrific, but he isn't here. The place is like a morgue. We haven't had even half the calls we usually get." Elaine lowered her voice. "Strictly between you and me, I think Colter should have closed the office. If not today, then last Friday. Elliot *was* a partner."

"I don't know why he didn't. It's a common convention, so you'd figure he'd tumble to it."

"Anyway, what I was getting at," Elaine continued, "if you want to kick back today, I could bring the Rolodex over, maybe at lunch?"

They arranged for Elaine to come at eleven-thirty, and Finny replaced the receiver. This way she could case out the booksellers Elliot had been in contact with. Barelli could gain access to it whenever he stumbled across it.

She shivered. She caught sight of herself in the mirror over the dresser. Her hair was sticking up in spikes all over her head and, wrapped in her towel, she looked like a refugee from a punker's ball. Nancy Drew, all grown up.

INTERLUDE

The South Platte River rolled through the heavy shade under the bridge, the arched views of the sun-drenched world outside shimmering like icons hung at either end.

Two men huddled against the curve of the bridge.

"Ain't it a beauty?" Bennie's breathy voice rippled into the hush.

Larkspur ran his hands over the silky finish of the box resting on his legs. His long fingers were grimy with old dirt, and one thumbnail had been torn off in a fight, but his hands were gentle and moved knowingly over the burnished surface.

"It's well made, but I can't see much in here."

Bennie cast a quick look around the shade cave. "Nobody can sneak up on us here. I got a match." He fumbled in one pocket of his olive wool overcoat and found a book of matches. He tore off one and struck it on the friction strip.

The smooth surface of the box shone in the feeble light. "It's nice," Larkspur said. "I'm pretty sure it's cedar."

"See the lock?" Bennie pointed to the metal circle under the lid. "Can you get it open?" The match fell to the ground in a tiny arc of light.

Larkspur shifted his weight to one hip and straightened his body so that he could reach into the pocket of his khaki work pants. He pulled out a Swiss Army knife. "There's an awl on this that should do it."

Bennie's eyes widened. "Where'd you get that?"

Larkspur inserted the awl into the lock. "Don't matter. Light another match." The knife gleamed in the fluttering light. "It's a simple one. You just have to shift the tongue." His hand twisted, and the lock released with a small click.

"Let me see." Bennie dropped the match, his hands eager for the box. He lifted it out of Larkspur's lap and set it on his own. "Here." He thrust the matches at Larkspur.

He started to lift the cover, then paused. "I wish Leila was here."

Larkspur scraped a match and watched as Bennie slowly lifted the lid. His face fell as he looked inside. "Looks like some old papers." He picked up a cardboard-bound bundle and held it in one hand. "Shit, I thought there'd be somethin' worth havin' in a box like this." His face twisted. "It's just old papers."

"Lemme see." Larkspur took the papers from Bennie's hand.

He lifted the makeshift cardboard cover over the papers. "Strike another match."

The angular writing seemed to move on the yellowed page

in the wavering light. *"The Death of Huckleberry Finn,"* he read aloud. "By Mark Twain."

The match dropped to the dirt and sputtered out.

"Bennie," Larkspur said, "I'll make you a trade."

CHAPTER
9

No one named Finn was in Elliot's Rolodex.

Everybody from Smith to Bronsky was, with Jones in between, to the tune of twenty-seven booksellers. Finny had thought to wait until she talked to Cronin before calling any of them, but as she went over what she'd heard him say to Marian, she realized that he couldn't have known where Elliot got the manuscript. He said he "thought" Elliot bought it the day he died. He couldn't have been there.

The longer she considered it, the more convinced she was that she should check out the booksellers in Elliot's file. What could it hurt? If she could find out who sold the manuscript to Elliot—what the manuscript was, for that matter—she'd be one up on Cronin when they met this afternoon. As Elliot had always said, deal from strength.

Finny had called all of the eight local dealers with no result. So far, none of the others she'd called had produced anything but increments in her telephone bill.

She glanced at the clock. One-seventeen. She could call the West Coast numbers before she met Cronin. If she had to call the numbers in England, she wouldn't be able to reach anyone until tomorrow morning anyway.

She referred again to the list she'd made. The next one was in Berkeley. After three rings, the phone was answered in a high-pitched, nasal voice. "Leander Books."

Here we go again. "Hello, my name is Finny Aletter. I'm calling from Denver about a possible customer of yours, Elliot Fulton. Do you know him?"

"Where did you get this number?" The voice was harsh and quick; Finny couldn't tell if it belonged to a man or a woman.

"From Mr. Fulton's files. Did he buy anything from you last week?"

"Why do you ask?"

If this creep did much business over the phone, Leander Books would soon be a thing of the past. "Look—is it Mr. Leander?—I'm just trying to get some information. Did Elliot Fulton buy anything from you last week?"

"I can't give out that kind of information without the permission of the customer."

Interesting. A simple 'no' would suffice if Elliot hadn't bought anything. "Oh, come on." Finny struggled to keep her voice unconcerned. "It's no big deal."

"Then why are you asking?"

"Maybe I'm interested in what Mr. Fulton bought," Finny ventured. "For myself, I mean." She grimaced at the phone.

The man said nothing.

Finny's muscles tightened. "Please tell me if you know anything. It's important."

After a pause, the breathy voice came again. "What did you say your name was?"

Finny told him.

"I'll have to call you back on this." The voice lowered. "I've got somebody here right now."

Finny gave him her telephone number and hung up. He sounded as though he might know something. She drew a star next to the name on the list. Berkeley. A university town would be a reasonable place to find a valuable manuscript.

If Leander Books were the source of the manuscript, couldn't she assume they had someone local to pass on the merchandise, possibly Mr./Ms. Finn. If she could figure out who Finn was, then she could discover what happened the day Elliot was killed: who saw him, who was present when the manuscript changed hands, who might have had reason to kill him. How simple.

Finny slid her feet into the slippers she'd shaken off under the table. She picked up her coffee mug and started for the kitchen.

She'd just pushed through the swinging door when the doorbell rang. She put her mug on the counter and went back out into the foyer.

The silhouette on the door's frosted oval window shifted, and the bell rang again.

She opened it enough to see Barelli looking straight at her. Before she could slam the door in his face, he shouldered his way in.

"Mind your manners," he said. "I need to talk to you."

Finny looked him over sourly. Tweed sports coat, gray

wool slacks. The pale yellow shirt and blue-green tie complemented both his eyes and his olive skin. Clear of eye, sound of limb, full of himself. She was aware of her worn jeans and ancient gray sweater.

"Well?"

"Your friend said you were sick," Barelli said. "You look it."

"Thanks." Finny grasped the doorknob more tightly and pulled the door farther open. "Thanks for dropping by to tell me."

Barelli grabbed the edge of the door. "No, Finny. You and I have some talking to do."

Finny glared up at him. She wouldn't be thrilled to see him any time, but now was definitely out. Leander Books would call back, and she couldn't talk to him with Barelli breathing down her neck. "What now, Lieutenant? More questions about Marian Fulton? Or maybe some words of wisdom about the perils of marriage?"

Barelli smiled tightly. "Cute, Finny. Can we sit down?"

"I'm very busy right now. What do you want?"

"It won't take long."

Finny shot him a glance of resentment and shoved the door shut.

Barelli glanced around the entryway, a look of surprise on his face. Finny followed his gaze over the warm wood tones and calm, flowered wallpaper. What did he expect—chrome high tech and current colors?

"What is it?" Finny demanded. "I told you, I'm very busy."

"Nice place," Barelli said. "I would've expected a townhouse in Glendale."

"Why?"

Barelli shrugged. "You're single, aren't you?"

"My hunting license expired. What d'you want?"

Barelli smiled at her sardonically. "Aren't you going to offer me some coffee or something? It's your turn, you know."

"You've enjoyed our conversations so much that you came by for a social call?" Finny's eyes drifted from his face to the coffee table in the living room framed in the doorway behind him. Elliot's Rolodex was lit artistically by the sunshine that poured through the west window.

"More likely a fencing session," he said dryly.

Finny forced her gaze back to Barelli. "There's some coffee in the kitchen."

"You think we could sit down?" He glanced toward the living room.

"In the kitchen."

Barelli followed her through the swinging door. The greenhouse windows drew him and he gazed out at her back yard.

He turned around slowly, his eyes admiring as they took in the room. "Nice. Very nice."

"Thanks." Finny gestured to the wicker chairs in the dining nook. "Sit down. I'll get the coffee."

Barelli eased his weight into the fragile-looking chair. "You sure this'll hold me?"

"It's stronger than it looks."

Barelli's eyes followed her movements as she stretched for a mug from a wall cabinet. "How long have you lived here?"

"About six years." She poured the coffee and carried the cups over to the table. "Okay, what do you want to talk about?"

"You do all this, or had it been done?" he asked idly.

"I did it." Finny sat down.

Barelli sipped the hot coffee. "You have any cream?"

"Will milk do?" At his nod she got up and went to the refrigerator.

"Who was your contractor?"

Finny brought the carton of milk to the table. "For what?"

"This." He gestured at the room around them.

"I told you, I did it."

Surprise flickered in Barelli's eyes. "You built this kitchen?"

"I had help with the plumbing and the wiring, but I did the rest," Finny said impatiently.

Barelli whistled. "You did a hell of a job."

"Thanks. What did you want to talk to me about?"

Barelli poured milk into his coffee and tasted it. "All right." He pulled a cigarette pack from his shirt pocket. "You got an ashtray?"

Her teeth clenched, Finny got up from the table once more.

Barelli lit a cigarette. "Thanks," he said when she put the ashtray on the table. He flicked nonexistent ashes into it.

Finny could feel the seconds ticking away. Why in God's name didn't he spit it out? Her hand tightened around her cup.

"I came to get Fulton's Rolodex."

Finny lifted the cup to her mouth and made herself sip slowly.

"A couple of my men picked up Fulton's papers after he died," Barelli said conversationally, "but they missed the Rolodex. Sloppy." He drew deeply on his cigarette and exhaled smoke in a stream. "I went by your office to get it this afternoon and had to spend a fair amount of time finding out where the damned thing was. Your friend, Mrs. Leyden, was reluctant to let me have that little piece of information."

Finny set her cup on the table. "Elaine was just doing me a favor."

"Oh, I'm sure she was. Now I'm hoping you'll do the same for me."

Finny met his eyes skeptically. "And what would that be?"

"Tell me what you're doing."

"I don't know what you mean."

"Sure you do." He stubbed out his cigarette. "I've been a cop for twenty years. You think you're the first person I've seen who wants to play detective?"

"I'm not playing—"

"Come on, Finny. We both know better." Barelli got up out of the chair and crossed to the coffee maker on the counter. He brought the carafe back to the table and topped off both of their cups, then replaced it. The wicker chair creaked under his weight as he sat down again. "You've got some wild idea that you can do something about Fulton's murder."

Finny shook her head. "That's not it."

"Then you tell me what it is, and tell me now. I don't mind sparring with you, but when you took evidence from Fulton's office, you upped the ante."

Her glance jerked back to his face at the warning in his voice. His eyes watched her steadily. "This is murder we're talking about."

The telephone rang.

Oh, shit. What could she say in front of Barelli? Finny pushed away from the table and went to the wall phone beside the kitchen cabinet.

A rough voice asked for Barelli.

Finny's eyes closed in relief. "Yes, just a minute. It's for you." She held out the receiver.

"Thanks. Barelli," he said into the telephone. His eyes narrowed as he listened. "What did it say? Anything else with the diary? Okay. I'll be there in a few minutes."

He hung the receiver on the wall unit, then looked at Finny. His face was empty of expression, his eyes cold once more. "I have to go. Would you get me Fulton's Rolodex and whatever else you took from his office?"

Finny flushed at his derisive tone. "Just a minute." She pushed through the swinging door with unnecessary force and strode through the dining room into the adjoining living room. He didn't have to make her feel like a petty thief. She pushed down the cover of the Rolodex and picked up her list of booksellers, folding it and stuffing it into her back pocket.

"Let me see that."

Finny whirled round. Barelli was watching her from the arched door to the entryway.

"It's mine," she said quickly.

Barelli walked toward her, his hand outstretched. "Let me see it."

"You have no right—"

"The hell I don't." Grabbing her shoulders, he spun her around and pulled the paper out of her pocket. Finny turned on him, fists clenched. Barelli pinned her with a icy glance. "Don't even think about it."

He unfolded the paper and read through the list, then looked up from it, a deep frown on his face. "You know about the manuscript?"

Finny's heart jerked. "Yeah, I know about the manuscript."

"How?"

"I overheard something."

"When?"

"Last night. At the Fulton house."

"I don't have time for Twenty Questions," Barelli growled. "Tell me what happened."

Finny glared at him. "I overheard Marian talking to someone who told her that Elliot bought a valuable manuscript the day he died. She didn't know a damned thing about it." She took a step toward him. "Have you got that? Marian was shocked to hear about it."

"Still on that kick, huh?" Barelli seemed to look right through her. "Who was it who told her about it?"

He wasn't going to get a shot at Cronin until she talked to him. Finny's eyes fell from his. "One of her guests. I didn't see who it was," she added rapidly in the face of Barelli's unwavering gaze. "I just happened to overhear—"

"You just happened to eavesdrop on the conversation, right?" One side of Barelli's mouth tightened. "Oh, yes, quite the little detective, aren't you?"

Damn him.

"So what's this?" He glanced back down at the list.

"Booksellers," Finny muttered. "I was trying to find out who sold Elliot the manuscript."

Barelli's eyes went flat and cold. "You've been calling these people? You asked them about the manuscript?"

Finny looked down at her clasped hands and wished violently for a drink.

"Christ!" Barelli's big hands clenched, crumpling the

paper. "I'd like to wring your neck." His voice was growing softer with each word. "I'm sure one of them copped to selling Fulton an unknown Mark Twain. Even gave you the provenance, right? Told you who stole it to begin with?"

Finny became aware that her mouth was hanging open. She carefully closed it. "An unknown Mark Twain?"

Barelli's eyes narrowed. "You didn't know?"

Finny's voice trembled. "No, just that Elliot bought something and that it could've been the motive for his murder."

"Talk about going off half-cocked. Do you realize where you stand right now? You show up the night Fulton's killed." He ticked off on his fingers. "You're found in his office the next morning, your name's on his calendar for the day he died." His hands dropped to his sides. "Why shouldn't I arrest you right now?"

"Because I didn't do it!"

Barelli glared at her. "Did you find out anything?"

"What?"

He waved the paper at her. "From the list."

"The one in Berkeley," Finny said. "Leander Books. I just talked to him. He seemed very nervous and was going to call me back."

"If he hasn't skipped town," Barelli muttered.

"He said he'd call me back."

"Bullshit." Barelli stepped to the table and reached for the phone. "You may have really blown this," he said as he rapidly punched in a number. "Larry, it's Chris. I need you to run a check on Leander Books, Berkeley, California." He gave him the number. "Go through Berkeley PD and ask for Mike Sinclair. Tell him we'd like him to nose around but to finesse it. No contact on their end unless it's called for. It has to do with the Fulton killing. I'll call him as soon as I can.

What? Oh, sure thing. Later." He replaced the receiver, then looked back at Finny with a grim expression.

Finny was suffering from the kind of anger that results from being in the wrong. The only cure is to hit back. "You're pretty high-handed with some other city's police department."

"I went to school in Berkeley," he said, and took a step toward her. "You'd better hope you haven't screwed this up. If I catch you anywhere near this case again, I'll stick you in jail so fast you'll have jet lag." He folded the list of booksellers and slid it into the inside pocket of his sports coat, then picked up the Rolodex and walked out of the room.

Finny followed him to the door. "How did you find out?" she thought to ask. "About the manuscript."

Barelli opened the door and glanced back at her. "Marian Fulton told me. She said she thought it might help in the investigation." His voice was dry as a martini.

"Don't you think that's enough to establish her innocence?" Finny demanded.

"Not necessarily." Barelli went out the door and closed it firmly behind him.

Finny lunged for the door and pulled it open. "Dammit, Barelli, what's with you?"

Barelli paused on the bottom step of the porch. "Stay out of it."

She stood on the porch as he got into his car and drove away. Damn him. If he thought he could dictate a bunch of crap to her and have her click her heels like some flunky . . .

She whirled around and went back into the house, slamming the door behind her. The bone-headed jerk still thought of Marian as a suspect, even though she was the one to tell him about the manuscript. Too bad he hadn't heard the shock in Marian's voice when Cronin told her about it. What would it take to make him see straight?

She caught sight of the clock on the dry sink. "Oh, hell," she muttered and headed up the stairs two at a time to change. She had exactly nineteen minutes until she was supposed to meet Cronin at the Marriott.

Finny asked for Cronin at the front desk. "Ms. Aletter?" responded the young woman at the counter. Her prominent cheekbones were highlighted with patches of plum-colored blusher, eclipsing her other features. "He said he'd meet you in the piano bar. Down the escalator and to your right."

Finny looked for him from the escalator. Snug little conversation islands of pillowy chairs and tiny tables radiated from the bar near the grand piano.

Cronin was sitting in an overstuffed love seat, his head bent over a magazine.

"Bart," she said as she came closer, "I'm sorry I'm late. I couldn't for the life of me find a parking place."

Cronin rose to his feet. In his blue pin-striped suit, he was businesslike and remote. "That's okay. I was glad to have a few minutes to myself."

He waved toward the bar as Finny sat down across from him. "It's good you could make it. I've been wanting to talk to you."

"Oh? What about?"

"Jennifer."

"What can I get you folks?" The bored, dark-haired waitress was overdressed for daytime. Her black tuxedo pants and tucked white dress shirt were better suited to shadows and romantic music drifting from the piano.

"A Coors draft," Finny said.

"Make it two. And could you bring me some matches?" Cronin pulled a cigarette pack from his coat pocket. "Have you talked to her today?"

"Jenn? No."

"I'm worried about her." The sapphire on his pinky ring sparkled as he pulled the cellophane strip from around the cigarette pack. "She's mentioned something rather disquieting: the possibility that Richard had something to do with Elliot's death."

Finny was aware of the canned music drifting from the speaker overhead and the rising voices from the two men seated at the bar. Where was the dramatic silence that such a pronouncement should bring? "Why would she think that?"

"I don't know." Cronin's serious eyes met hers steadily. "That's one of the reasons I'm worried. If she knows something, she ought to tell the police."

"Kind of hard when you're talking about turning in your brother, don't you think? Here come our drinks."

The waitress set glasses on the table and made quick change for the five Cronin handed her. The dollar tip he left on the tray elicited a smile, and she slapped down a book of matches with a little flourish.

Finny watched her move back toward the bar. Bored she might be, but she probably didn't have to concern herself with murder or missing manuscripts. Maybe she'd be up for trading places. "Why are you telling me this?"

Cronin glanced at the strip of cellophane in his hands.

"Somebody needs to know about it. You're a friend of the family. I guess I figured you might have some perspective on the thing. I don't know how seriously to take it."

Finny let out her breath in a sigh. "Sure thing. I know she's scared of Richard and that he's been drinking too much and acting like a jerk. But that's all I know."

"You're not aware of any reason he might have killed Elliot?"

Finny shook her head. There was a damned big gulf between father-son friction and murder.

"You worked with the guy," Cronin said. "Do you know why anybody else might've wanted to kill him?"

Finny took a swallow of beer, noting with interest the earnestness in Cronin's light gray eyes.

"No." She set her glass down. "You knew Elliot, too. Who in the book-collecting world could have had it in for him?"

"Don't imagine I haven't thought about it." Cronin shook his head and tapped a cigarette out of the pack. "I can't guess why anybody might have killed him."

His nose didn't grow a centimeter. Finny kept her face expressionless, but her insides starting doing their imitation of Jell-o. She wouldn't mention the manuscript to him now, not even for an accurate crystal-ball forecast of the market for the next fiscal year.

"I guess we'll have to leave it to the police to figure out," she said. Barelli should hear this.

"It's hard as hell to stand by and watch." Cronin lit his cigarette and blew out the match. "I care about Jennifer. It's hard to see her like this."

"I know." Jesus, all Jenn needed was a ring-tailed bastard like this. What the hell was he up to? Then the thought, like a sidewinder undulating across sand, squirmed across her mind. Could Cronin have killed Elliot?

"You never think that something like this can happen to anybody you know." She speeded up her consumption of beer. "I hope the police figure it out fast. Sorry to drink and run, but I need to get back."

Cronin's forehead wrinkled. "Wait a minute. What was it you wanted to talk to me about?" His mouth curled at the nonplussed expression on Finny's face. "You did call me."

Finny smiled with effort. What, what, what? "You already took care of it. When I asked you about book collectors. You know, if somebody might have had reason to kill Elliot."

He nodded. "I guess we both struck out."

"Guess so. Oh, well, at least we suited up. You know—sometimes you win, sometimes you lose, but you always—"

"Suit up," Cronin finished. His eyes were puzzled. "At least we care enough to try, right?"

"Right." Finny stood up. "I hate to run, but I really have to. Thanks for the beer."

"Sure thing. I'm sure I'll be seeing you."

"Yeah. 'Bye."

It was all she could do to keep from running out of the bar. Cronin waved to her as she rode up the escalator to the main lobby. She lifted her hand in an anemic response.

What the hell had she got herself into?

The telephone was ringing when she came through the back door of her house. Leander Books, no doubt.

"Hello."

"Finny, it's Elaine."

Finny relaxed. "Elaine, I—"

"Just listen. I can't talk long." Elaine's voice was nearly a whisper. "Julia Simons is dead."

"What?"

"Gloria found her. I told you—she was worried about her when she didn't show up for work. Wait a minute."

Finny heard muffled voices in the background. Then Elaine came back on the line. "I can't talk any more," she whispered. "Colter's going ape-shit around here."

"Hold it," Finny said sharply. "What happened to her?"

"Finny, she killed herself."

CHAPTER

10

*F*inny put down the phone and walked into the breakfast nook. This would go into the record books as one of the all-time lousy Mondays. Outside a wind was blowing the naked branches of the honey locust tree. She hadn't pulled off the dead flowers after the first frost; their stiff stalks had broken under the weight of the winter snows and remained only as a jagged stubble.

Suicide. Julia was angry last night, even desperate, but to kill herself. . . . She was so busy striking out at people, you would've thought there'd be nothing left to turn against herself.

Finny leaned her forehead against the cold glass of the window. Julia dead. Elliot dead. Was somebody else on the list? Or was it tragic coincidence? Or was it—what was it? She stared with hatred out the window at the dried flower stalks, then kicked off her slippers and padded into the utility room off the kitchen. She found her old tennis shoes in the broom closet and sat on the floor to put them on. She had just opened the door to go outside when the phone rang again. Finny glanced back over her shoulder at it and started to go out the door. Then she stopped and went back to the phone.

"Hello."

The breathy voice was familiar now. Leander Books. "Ms. Aletter?"

"Yes."

"We spoke earlier—about Elliot Fulton." The edge of fear was gone.

"Yes."

"You said you were interested in what Mr. Fulton might have bought."

"That's right."

"I assume you have enough . . . wherewithal to be . . . how shall we say it? Taken seriously?"

Finny's mouth twisted. "You bet I do."

"So you're interested in being put on our . . . mailing list?"

"That depends," Finny said deliberately. "Did you sell Elliot Fulton a manuscript last week?"

"Let's just say that Mr. Fulton has been a client of ours in the past."

The anger licking at Finny's mind flared. "Let's just say that's not good enough. Did you or didn't you?"

The sound of the receiver being hung up on the other end was a soft click in her ear. She'd blown it, Finny realized sickly.

Finny slammed the phone down and crossed the room.

She went out onto the porch and pulled the door shut behind her.

She looked at the yard from the top step. It lay unawakened, as always this time of year, sporting the remnants of the last growing season, much like a room left uncleaned after a raucous party. Newspapers and wrappers had blown against the privacy fence she'd built last spring.

Finny took a rake out of the garage and leaned it against the side of the house. Squatting on her heels, she started pulling up dead plants. Snapdragons, marigolds, weeds. Or what was left of them. Their yellowed stalks were sharp against her skin as she tugged them from the dry, cold soil. A musty scent rose from the plants as their roots pulled free. She finished the small flower bed at the corner of the house and grabbed the rake. Holding it like a broom, she swept the dead plants into a pile in the middle of the backyard.

A jet thundered overhead, banking sharply as it climbed for altitude into the gunmetal gray clouds to the south. The gradual quiet in its wake was broken by the restless barking of a dog down the street.

Finny propped the rake back against the wall and flexed her hands. No telling where she'd put her gloves last fall. She sucked at the blood in the crease of one index finger, then started again. She wanted all of the flower beds clear, rid of the brittle stubble and dead leaves and trash that had blown in on the wind. After that she could think what to do.

She pulled down the dried morning glory vines that were twisted around the drainpipe, intertwined, doubling back over themselves in an undulating pattern that had produced a vertical mass of sky blue blossoms up the side of the house at summer's end. The dried remains were a fretwork of age against the ochre brick of the wall.

She moved faster, grasping the dead stalks of hollyhock that jutted out of the center of the living plant. She tugged at them, then tried to break them off at the bottom, but they were fibrous and tough and wouldn't snap. She wrapped the stalks around her hands and braced her foot against the wall of the house, pulling again as hard as she could. The sharp stalks tightened around her hands and cut into her skin. She jerked once more and the plant came up, roots and all, and Finny fell back onto the grass, loose dirt flying into her face.

She threw the plant away from her, sobbing curses under her breath. She spat dirt from her mouth and cradled her stinging hands under her arms. They hurt, she hurt, all over.

Finny got on her hands and knees and pushed herself up. The sun was cradled in pink and gray clouds on the horizon. The billowing shapes frothed above the dark purple mountains. How celestial, she thought savagely. All that was missing were the trumpets. She looked around the yard for more debris.

She bent over the remains of the pansies and primroses. Damn Julia. She threw rotted pansy plants at the big pile of trash. You don't kill yourself. You seal off the hurt, you get stubborn, you fight back. Finny wiped her nose on the back of her hand. You damned well fight back.

The wind came up a little, stirring through the mound of debris. A leaf or two skittered off the top of the pile and landed on the grass. Finny laid the rake across the pile and headed toward the alley for a garbage can.

She lifted the latch and swung the gate open, wincing at the squeak of the hinges. A gust of wind pulled the gate out of her hold, and she grabbed for it automatically, coming up against the woman who stood next to the row of garbage cans along the fence.

"Oh, I'm sorry," Finny said breathlessly. She took a step back in embarrassment. "The wind took the gate out of my hand . . ." Her voice died as she recognized the woman. Her gray coat was crookedly buttoned now, but the collar of the pink flowered dress peeped above the food-stained velvet lapels. Her long white hair whipped in the fitful wind. Her blue eyes were vacant, as though knowledge and experience had left nothing behind.

"I saw you this morning," Finny said.

The woman's stare dropped. "Goin' home." Her voice had the plummy, cracked sound that Finny associated with grandmothers and witches.

Finny smiled and moved back another step. She gestured toward the woman's grocery cart, which was nearly full of cans and bottles. "It looks like you found a lot of stuff today."

The woman looked at the basket. "People throw away things instead of gettin' their money out of 'em."

"Maybe they don't have time to trade them in," Finny ventured.

"Time! People throw away good things. Won't even take time to fix 'em. Just toss 'em out."

Finny reached for one of the garbage cans and started to heft it. "Well, I guess I'd better get back to—"

"We're headin' for another depression," the old woman said dreamily. "Back before the Crash people throwed away good stuff, couldn't be bothered with it if it got busted. Then after it happened, they would've gave a lot for what they throwed away."

Finny edged back toward the open gate. "I guess you're right. I—"

"I find all kinds of stuff, just sittin' in these here cans." She

131

reached into her basket, pawing through the cans and bottles "Look." She held up her prize. "There ain't nothin' wrong with this can opener. Bennie and me can use it. Needs a little sharpenin's all." She shook her head. "Somebody just throwed it out."

"I've got to be going now," Finny said firmly. "Nice talking to you." She carried the garbage can through the gate and shut it behind her. She could still hear the old woman talking.

"Finny, what are you doing out here?"

Finny wheeled around. Jennifer Fulton stood in the open back doorway.

"How'd you get into my house?" Finny demanded.

Jennifer looked taken aback. "The front door was open a bit. I yelled for you and got a little worried when you didn't answer. I was just looking for you."

Finny remembered slamming the door when she ran in to answer the phone. It must not have latched properly. She hunched her shoulders against the sharp breeze that snaked around the corner of the house. "I'm sorry—wait a minute." She carried the garbage can to the pile she'd made and began loading it. She had to finish what she'd started.

Jennifer closed the door behind her and came down the steps into the yard. She was wearing snug jeans and a short pink ski parka. "Would you rather be alone?"

"No, I just—dammit." Finny dropped a wad of weeds into the can and peered at the palm of one hand. "I wish I knew where the hell my gloves were." She pulled out some stickers. "I'll have to use a needle on a couple of these."

Jennifer watched her pick up the leaves and plants. "Isn't it kind of cold to work in the yard?"

"Yeah, it's cold." Finny put the last load of trash into the can. "Let me go set this out in the alley." She opened the gate once more and peered around it. The old woman was farther down the alley. Finny set the garbage can back in its place and returned to the yard.

"You want to come inside?" she asked Jennifer.

"Okay. Uh, I was kind of hoping I could talk you into having dinner with me."

Finny walked up the back porch steps and held the door open for Jennifer. "Go out, you mean?" She closed the door and followed her into the kitchen. "I'm awfully tired, Jenn. It's been a hell of a day."

"I could really use the company," Jenn said in a rush. "I mean, if you're too tired, I understand."

She'd been crying. Her father was dead, and unless Cronin had lied about that, too, she was afraid her brother might be involved in it. She was entitled to cry. "A bad day for you, too, huh?"

Jennifer produced a smile. "Yeah."

Fatigue dragged at Finny. She thought longingly of sinking into a tub full of hot water and letting every thought leach out of her mind. The day had lasted forever and had too many repercussions to think about.

The pleading in Jennifer's eyes made the decision for her. "Okay, but I don't want to stay out too late."

Jennifer nodded. "Whatever. We could just grab a bite somewhere. I'm not dressed for anything fancy."

Finny glanced down at herself. Her gray wool slacks were grass-stained and spotted with the detritus of dried leaves. She'd never changed her clothes after meeting Cronin. "They wouldn't let me into a dogfight. I'll go get cleaned up." She paused at the foot of the stairs. "Have a drink. I'll be ready in a few minutes."

"Thanks a lot, Finny."

"Don't worry about it."

"He was yelling at Mother, and when I walked in he lit into me for spending so much time with Bart," Jennifer charged bitterly. "He's throwing his weight around as if he has the right to."

"But that's all he's done?" So far Jennifer hadn't said anything to substantiate what Cronin had told her. Richard had never been known for his sweet disposition, and from what Jenn had told her tonight, he hadn't changed in that regard, but there was a whole lot of difference between coming on too strong and killing his father. What reason could Cronin have for exaggerating Jenn's feelings? God, she was so tired of complications.

Finny glanced around the restaurant. It was one of her favorites, a small Greek place not too far from her house. Its dark red vinyl booths and low ceiling created a cavelike coziness in which to consume the cheap, plentiful food. Tonight most of the customers had opted for home cooking. The cashier, built like an opera diva, had only Finny and Jennifer and the stoned couple in the corner to watch for entertainment.

"Then he told me I could take his car and drive to hell in it." Jennifer was making fast work of her third glass of wine.

"So you came to my place."

Jennifer set down the glass with a thump. "Same thing, as

far as he's concerned." She glanced up at Finny. "You know he's never liked you."

"Yeah, I know. What I never figured out was why."

Jenn looked back into her glass. "Quite a puzzle, isn't it?"

Finny lifted her glass and drank the rest of her wine. "What do you say we go home? I'm so tired I can't see straight."

Jennifer's gaze met Finny's. Her face was flushed, and there was an odd, reckless look about her. "Why is it you've never married?"

Finny stared at her. "Why do you ask?"

Jenn's shrug was elaborate. "Just wondering, I guess. It seems kind of strange."

Finny had the sinking feeling that all the wine Jenn had drunk had not been a good idea. "I never found the right guy, I guess."

"You're awfully attractive, and smart," Jennifer went on. "Daddy always said so. I would've thought that you'd have found somebody a long time ago."

Finny smiled tightly. "Now you sound like my mother."

Jennifer's eyes glittered. "I've often thought of you as a sister. Did you know that?"

Finny shook her head.

"You've always felt like family." Jenn's voice had an edge to it. "I've always felt so close to you."

Finny stood up. "Let's get out of here." She dug into her purse for her billfold and threw down a tip for the waitress. She crossed the room to the cashier's stand.

"We need our check," she said. "We're in a hurry."

The woman's eyebrows were dark and thick and a spectrum away from her bleached hair. "I'll get that for you right away." She eased her rear off the barstool behind the counter and ambled to the open kitchen door. "Angie, you got these ladies' check?"

Angie brought the check and the bill was paid. "You come back a see us real soon, now," called the cashier.

"Good night." The bell on the door jangled like frayed nerves as Finny went outside, Jenn following.

"How much do I owe you?" she asked stiffly.

"My treat." The cold air hit Finny in the face. She buttoned her leather coat and pulled her gloves out of her pockets. "The temperature must have dropped twenty degrees."

The sound of their heels against the concrete sidewalk was sharp in the still, cold air.

"Finny, I don't want to go home."

Finny took her keys out of her bag and continued toward her car. "I've got to. I'm tired and so are you. Do you want me to drive you home, or do you want to spend the night?"

"I can drive myself home," Jennifer began belligerently.

"Forget it. You've had a lot to drink, and you're exhausted." Finny opened the passenger door and held it for Jennifer. "Get in before we freeze our buns off."

Finny went around the car to open her own door and slid onto the seat. She shivered and started the car. "Okay, what's your choice? My place or yours?"

"I'd better go home. Richard was going out, and Mom's kind of nervous about being alone after dark."

Finny let out a silent sigh of relief. Even if Jennifer had the key to every puzzling thing that was going on right now, she couldn't handle it tonight. She drove the car away from the curb.

Jenn looked at Finny. Her face was illuminated dimly by the dashboard lights. "What about Richard's car?"

"Get it tomorrow."

Finny drove automatically through the desultory traffic of Speer Boulevard. She would sleep, and in the morning she would know what to do. No playing with fire tonight. No _in vino veritas_ crap for her.

She pulled into the circular driveway in front of Jennifer's house and stopped the car.

"Thanks, Finny."

Finny nodded. "Get some sleep."

Jennifer gazed at her sadly. "I always did love you." She was nearly crying.

"I love you, too," Finny said thickly. She leaned across the gear shift lever to hug her, but Jenn pulled away. The front door to the house opened, spilling light out onto the steps.

The man in the doorway paused for an instant, then strode across the grass toward them. He jerked open the passenger door and grabbed Jennifer's arm. "Get in the house," he ordered and pulled her out of the car.

"Richard," Jennifer began hotly.

"What the hell do you think you're doing?" Finny blazed.

"Do what I said," Richard snapped. He leaned down to look in at Finny. Menace came off him in waves. "You leave my sister alone. We don't have to put up with you anymore. Dad's death had a few fringe benefits."

Finny's heart was racing. "Richard, why are you—"

"You know damned well why!" Richard hit the roof of the car with his fist. "You were one of his women, you goddamned bitch. Don't you ever come to this house again." He slammed the door with all his strength and wheeled around.

Jennifer stood motionless behind him. He grabbed her arm and pulled her toward the house.

Finny sat unmoving. *One of his women.* How many had there been? How many were there? Did Marian know? When Richard looked back at her car, she let out the clutch too fast and stalled the engine. Her hands were shaking so badly that it was hard to turn the key to restart the car. She drove blindly out of the driveway into the street.

Mercifully, there were no other cars coming. Eyes full of tears, she slowed the car to a crawl. "My God," she whispered. "My God."

Finny slid her key into the lock and opened the front door. The foyer was softly lit by a small lamp on the oak chest beside the stairs. She closed the door behind her and, with difficulty, shot the bolt beneath the knob. She leaned against the door, her head bent.

She wanted a drink more than anything else in the world. She was halfway across the living room when she froze. All of the books from the bookcases on either side of the fireplace were scattered on the floor. The sofa cushions were propped against the coffee table, their covers unzipped. The blanket chest under the window was open, its contents piled in front of it.

Her mind flashed the question: Surely I didn't leave it like this? And just as quickly answered it: someone had been here. Here in her house. The air around her felt different, tainted.

Finny moved forward toward the coffee table. She couldn't get enough air into her lungs. Her hand was shaking as she reached for the phone.

She heard a sound from the kitchen.

Finny didn't move. She strained to listen, but she couldn't hear anything except the pounding of her heartbeat in her ears. She straightened up slowly. She backed away from the table. Her heel touched something, and she turned quickly. A sofa cushion.

She moved toward the foyer, every nerve ending aware of the dark archway to the dining room and kitchen. Barely breathing, she edged toward the front door. Her hand grasped the knob, and she leaned against the door to ease the bolt from its sheath.

She pulled the door open, every second expecting someone to grab at her and pull her back. Her hand was wet with sweat and it slipped on the doorknob. She darted through the narrow gap and eased the door shut behind her.

Her breath was coming in short, hard gasps. She had to hurry. She nearly tripped on the porch steps. She would call the police. One of the neighbors would let her use the phone.

Finny ran awkwardly to the sidewalk. Her legs weren't working right. The shadows cast by the street light enveloped her. The night threatened, her familiar surroundings had changed.

She looked at the street, saw her car. She could drive to a phone, go to an all-night store. Before she'd taken two steps she remembered. No keys. The keys were in the house.

Her eyes went desperately to the houses on either side of hers. No lights in one, a porch light on the other. She fell going up the steps to the house with the light, coming down hard on one knee. She scrambled up, barely noticing the pain. Her frantic hands found the doorbell, and she leaned on it. They have to be home, she thought desperately. Please let them be home.

She kept looking over her shoulder while she waited. When the door finally opened, she jerked around. The balding man who stood there was wrapped haphazardly in a dark blue robe. "What's going on?" he demanded.

Finny's voice came out in a tight whisper. "Somebody's in my house. Next door. Can I call the police?"

He stepped back from the doorway and motioned her in. "You hurt?"

Finny shook her head. "Just scared."

"Les, what is it?" The dark man on the stairs saw Finny as she came in. "What's the matter?"

"The telephone's in here," Les said to Finny. "She said someone's in her house."

"Oh, my God."

Finny barely heard him. She dialed the emergency number and concentrated on keeping her hands from shaking. When the operator answered, she gave the necessary information.

"And where are you now?" the operator asked finally.

"Next door, the house just north of mine."

"There'll be someone there right away." The line went dead.

Finny replaced the receiver and turned. "They're on their way." She shivered. "Is it all right if I wait here?"

"Of course," said the dark man. "Come over here and sit down."

The police found no one in the house or in the surrounding neighborhood. Finny talked to one of the uniformed police officers while the other went through the rest of the house to try to get usable fingerprints.

"I doubt that we'll get anything," the older one said laconically. His face was ordinary, even kind, except for his eyes. He looked at Finny with a tiredness that went all the way through him. "He came through the back window, and there wasn't anything on the glass or the frame. Probably wore gloves. Most of 'em do that now, even the kids. TV."

Finny nodded. What would she do when they left?

The cop wrote more on the form he held in his lap. "So, nothing besides the TV band radio is missing?"

Finny shook her head. "I haven't been upstairs yet."

"Let's do it."

The officer led the way up the stairs, Finny limping in his wake. Her knee had stiffened from the fall on the neighbors' steps. "Got anything?" he asked his partner, who was coming out of Finny's bedroom.

He was a young, open-faced blond. He shook his head, his expression troubled. "A couple of blurred prints on the bathroom door, but nothing usable." He pulled a cigarette out of his shirt pocket. "Sure is a mess in there."

Finny stood in the open doorway and looked at the shambles of her bedroom.

The drawers had been pulled from the dresser and upended. Their contents were strewn on the rug between the dresser and the bed. The mirror on the closet door hung crookedly from one corner. The mattress was half off the bed frame, and the bedding lay in a pile beside it.

Finny stepped hesitantly into the room.

"You want to see if anything's missing?" said one of the officers behind her.

Finny didn't answer. She stepped over the cranberry comforter and picked up her pale yellow nightshirt lying on the floor beside the bed. The soft material had been ripped nearly in two. She watched as from a distance as her hands began to shake again.

"What's going on, Forrest?"

"Hi, Chris. B and E, with nothing much missing so far. Nothing for your beat."

Finny turned her head. Barelli stood in the doorway watching her. She was surprised at how glad she was to see him. Her eyes fell again to the nightshirt in her hands.

"You guys finished here?"

"Except for the final list of what's missing," the older cop said.

"I need to talk to her. I can get the list to you later if you want to head out."

"Sure thing, Chris."

Finny heard their footsteps on the stairs. Barelli moved across the room, then stood in front of her. The small beads of moisture on his wool overcoat reflected the overhead light.

"Your coat's wet."

"It just started snowing."

"Oh." The shaking in her hands had extended to the rest of her. She dropped the nightshirt to the floor and wrapped her arms around herself.

"Finny."

She glanced up at him.

"You okay?"

Finny shook her head.

"You're not hurt?"

"Could you do me a favor?" Her voice shook. "Could you maybe hold me before I fall into pieces here?"

His arms slid around her, and he pressed her head against the rough fabric of his coat. "It's all right, Finny," he said. He touched her hair. "It's all right."

"No, it's not," she whispered.

INTERLUDE

*I*t was cold.

Outside the shelter, street people had gathered early. Beds were few. The difference between sleeping on a mattress and having to stretch out on the floor was decided by who got there first.

The shambling drunk who pushed into the line near the door must have figured he was big enough to get away with it, if he was up to figuring anything at all. The small black man behind him saw it differently. He jumped on the invader's back and commenced punching.

The rest edged back enough to give them room, keeping their places in line.

Bennie skirted the action, approaching the knot of critics bad-mouthing the fighters.

"What's goin' on?"

A man in ragged fatigues with a greasy blond pony tail turned. "Well, if it ain't little Bennie. Where's your retard girlfriend? She dump you for a better time?"

His giggle followed Bennie through the shifting circle around the combatants, whose battle had deteriorated into a clumsy dance.

"Tulsa Joe gonna get his ass whipped." The stocky Chicano next to Bennie spat on the sidewalk. "He's stoned out of his gourd."

Bennie shivered inside his coat. Good thing Leila wasn't here. She'd get all nervous, and they'd change her medicine again at the halfway house. She didn't even want to talk to him when they done that and then he spent all his nights alone instead of only some.

Tulsa Joe threw himself at his opponent and brought them both up hard against the front row of spectators. The crowd gave way.

"Jesus Christ, those assholes can't fight worth shit." The grizzled black man who came toward the back shook his head and spat. "Ain't worth stickin' around to see." He caught sight of Bennie and smiled, his grin gap-toothed. "Bennie, my man."

Bennie smiled weakly and edged back. "Louis, howya doin'?"

Louis grabbed Bennie's hand and pumped it with good humor. "I hear you comin' into some money, man. You wouldn't have a little . . . remembrance for your old buddy, now would you?"

Bennie kept his face blank. "Where'd you hear that?"

"Some uptown dude be lookin' for you, man. He say you got a box worth some money. He askin' all about you."

Bennie's rodent features twitched. "Was he the heat?"

Louis was hurt. "Now, Bennie, would I go talkin' to the Man?"

"What'd he say?"

"Jus' he lookin' for a man with a red scarf who gots a box, that's all. Somebody else told him your name."

"And who was that?"

Louis's voice flattened. "I ain't no snitch, Bennie."

"Jesus, Louis, if you see him, don't tell him you seen me. I gotta hang loose a while."

Louis nodded. "No problem, my man. But do you think you might have a little somethin' to carry me for a bit?" He smiled as he felt the bill slipped into his hand. "I never see you no more, Bennie, you jus' disappeared."

Bennie walked away from the shelter, leaving the light and noise behind. He scuttled down the dirty street, casting quick glances over his shoulder. It must have been the man in the alley. "Jesus God," he muttered, "he must've seen me pick it up."

But he'd went off and left it. Ain't fair to keep after something when you left it behind.

Some uptown dude, Louis said. Bennie hunched his shoulders and moved faster down the pitted sidewalk. Somebody who knew his name and where to ask around for him. And he'd sold the box today.

CHAPTER

11

"You lead an eventful life." Barelli's voice rumbled above Finny's ear. "Do you know what's missing?"

Finny kept her eyes closed and savored the feel of his arms. "Just a TV band radio from the kitchen."

"That's it?"

"So far." He showed no sign of letting go, so it was up to her. She pulled out of his arms. "I'm okay."

Barelli whistled absently between his teeth as he prowled around the room. The drawer he picked up fell apart, the bottom of it dropping to the floor. "Thorough, but no finesse," he muttered.

"What?"

"Whoever searched this place."

"Searched it? What are you talking about?"

Barelli glanced at her as pulled open the closet door. "Come on, Finny." He knelt to sift through the clothing and papers on the floor. "You said it yourself. Nothing's missing."

"The radio."

He stood up. "All this for a lousy radio?" He shook his head. "Too much for too little. There's all kinds of stuff downstairs that would've been easy to fence. The TV, your sound equipment . . ."

The logic of it frightened her. "Maybe he got interrupted. I heard somebody when I first got here."

Barelli shrugged. "Maybe. But why would anybody take time to go through all this stuff instead of just popping what was downstairs? Burglary's an in and out proposition. You don't stick around to fondle the possessions."

He had a way with words. Finny's eyes searched the floor for the torn nightgown.

Barelli came toward her. "You just turned the same color as your sweater." His hand was dark against the green wool as he took her arm. "You want to sit down?"

Finny cast a wild look around the room. "Sure, I'll just clear a little space here, and—"

"Wait a minute." He pushed the mattress back onto its box springs and kicked aside the welter of bedding on the floor. "Here."

She sat. Barelli looked down at her, his eyes red-rimmed, the dark stubble of his beard showing through tanned skin. "Do you have anything to drink in the house?"

"Downstairs." She started to get up.

His hand on her shoulder kept her from rising. "I'll get it. Where is it?"

"In the dining room, on the sideboard."

The stairs creaked as he went down.

Finny surveyed the room. Not a bad arrangement, really.

Everything was within sight, easily reached. She'd just have to kick the clothes around a little to find what she wanted. They might get a little wrinkled, but what the hell. Wrinkled was in.

When Barelli came into the room a few minutes later, a glass in each hand, Finny was sorting through the closet, jerking garments onto hangers with exaggerated precision.

"Finny."

A blouse dropped out of her hands. "I didn't hear you."

"Sorry." He gave her a glass and lifted his own to his lips, watching her over the edge as he drank. She was channeling her fear into anger.

She swallowed a healthy dose of liquor and coughed.

"Slow down," said Barelli. "That's good brandy."

"I can get more." Finny looked up at him challengingly. "What makes you think somebody searched the house?"

"Sit down before you fall down." He settled himself on the bed, leaning against the headboard, extending his long legs onto the mattress.

Finny went around to the other side of the bed and sat on the edge. "I'm sitting. Tell me."

Barelli rested his head against the headboard and closed his eyes. "Your place is turned upside down but nothing to speak of is taken. Either you've got an incompetent thief or somebody was looking for something."

"But what? What could I have that anybody would want?"

Barelli's eyes opened a crack. "How about an unknown Twain manuscript?"

Finny's stomach settled down into her knees. "That doesn't make any sense."

"Why?"

149

"Why? If Elliot was killed because of the manuscript, then the killer would have taken the damned thing."

"Not if it wasn't there." He drained his glass.

"Shit." Finny rubbed at the ache in one temple. She was beginning to feel like Barelli's straight man. His punch lines sucked. "If it wasn't there, then why was Elliot killed?"

"Maybe he wouldn't give it up, maybe he tried to get rough, I don't know. But I'll bet you dollars to doughnuts that our murderer doesn't have the manuscript." His gaze wandered over her. "Or at least didn't the night of the murder."

"What makes you think that's even a possibility?"

Barelli gestured toward the room at large. "This house."

"But—"

"The sofa cushions are unzipped, Finny. Pictures have been pulled off the walls, the drawers emptied and pulled apart. What kind of a burglar does that?"

Finny shook her head. "There's no reason for anybody to think I have it."

"Wrong. You were close to Fulton. You were at his house the night he was killed."

"I got there after you did!"

"How many people know that?" He set his empty glass onto the floor beside the bed. "Did the guy at the bookstore call back?"

"Yes. He didn't tell me anything," she added at his frown. "If he had I'd have called you."

"What did he say?"

"He wanted to know if I had enough money to get into the game." She answered the question in his eyes. "I told him I'd heard about Elliot's manuscript and was interested in the same kind of thing."

"Jesus," Barelli muttered. "I suppose you gave him your mailing address and said you'd keep in touch."

"I gave him my phone number," Finny snapped, "and when he fiddle-farted around, I got mad and told him to tell me if he knew anything. He hung up, and we'll probably never hear from him again. Okay?"

Barelli shook his head. "Berkeley says he hasn't made a move yet, but he's had time to find out Fulton's dead and to put together a little Maltese Falcon action around the manuscript. Since you so obligingly furnished him with your phone number, therefore your address, he's probably dealt you into the game whether you like it or not."

"Why should he? If he already sold it to Elliot, why would he do anything but sit tight?"

"Finny," Barelli said gently, "we are talking big-time bucks here. Odds are that whoever sold the manuscript to Elliot was just a middleman, doing it for a commission. Would you pass up a chance to have another go-round with that kind of money?"

"Sure, thanks to the SEC." Finny frowned. "But I still don't get it. I was the one asking questions. If I had the goddamned manuscript, why would I do that?"

Barelli pulled a pack of Marlboros out of his pocket and got a cigarette going. "What does he have to lose?"

Finny shrugged dispiritedly.

"If I had anything to do with something as hot as this manuscript," Barelli continued, "and I found out the new owner was dead, I'd start with whatever information I had and go with it. The guy has your phone number. It's a place to start."

Finny had to admit that what he said made sense, as far as it went. She sighed. "Maybe it was Finn."

"Huh?"

"The name on Elliot's calendar. Remember, thanks to Greg you thought it was me."

"Oh, yeah." He didn't sound convinced that it hadn't been.

Finny yawned. "What time is it?"

"Nearly eleven."

"It's got to be later than that."

"Nope. You have to work tomorrow?"

She nodded.

"You'd better get some sleep."

Finny stood up. "Oh, sure. After I spend some time thinking about the faceless Finn and the long arm of Leander Books."

He looked at her searchingly and sighed. "You're right. Bad timing." He glanced around the room irritably. "Do you have anyplace else you can sleep?"

"There's a guest room across the hall."

"Come on." He walked her out of her bedroom and turned off the light.

They went into the spare room together. The very act of walking through the door made her feel better. It had barely been touched, with only a few books out of place. It was a comfortable room, its creamy white wallpaper sprinkled with small pink rosebuds, the windows' darkly varnished shutters contrasting sharply with the cream woodwork. The small ruffled lamp on the bedside table made a pool of light in the shadowy room. It was an island of sanity.

Barelli closed the shutters against the night and pulled down the blue chenille spread and blankets of the double bed. The crisp white of the pillowcases touched off a memory of childhood. She knew the scent they would have.

Finny kicked off her shoes and sat on the bed. "Thanks, Barelli, for walking me through this—what are you doing?"

Barelli had hung his overcoat on the back of the flowered easy chair next to the window. He sat down and tugged at his tie. "I'm not going to leave you in this house alone," he said gruffly. "You're coming apart at the seams as it is."

The room was very silent as he undid the top button of his shirt and settled back in the chair.

"Thanks," Finny said softly.

"Turn out the light."

She pushed the lamp switch and lay back on the bed, pulling the blankets over her. "How long has it been since you slept?" she asked after a minute.

"I'll be all right."

"Well, at least come stretch out on the bed. I'm too tired to rape you."

"Promises, promises." His voice was weary.

"Come on, Barelli. There's plenty of room."

"Okay." He came across the room and around to the other side. The edge of the mattress sagged when he sat on it to take off his shoes. "Do you snore?"

"No. Do you?"

"Let me know." Barelli stretched out on his side of the bed. "Get some sleep."

"You too." Her eyes opened. "I forgot to lock up."

"I did when I was downstairs."

Before she could sort out the reasons she felt so at ease with him now, Finny was asleep.

* * *

Finny rushed awake, her heart pounding with fear. There were tears on her cheeks, and she could still hear the frenzied shouting from Richard Fulton. She made a small, despairing sound in the dark.

"It's okay," rumbled Barelli beside her. "Relax."

Finny let out the breath she'd taken in at the first sound of his voice and lay back on the pillow. "I forgot you were here."

Barelli shifted onto his side. "Last night was tough on you. Plenty of reason for bad dreams."

"I—thanks for staying." Her voice broke. "I appreciate it."

He put his arm across her. "It'll be okay, Finny."

She turned her face into her pillow, struggling to keep from crying aloud.

"What is it?" His hand stroked her hair. "Why the tears now?"

"Oh, God," Finny sobbed. "He hated me. If he could have killed me he would have."

His hand stilled. "What're you talking about? Who would have killed you?"

"Richard Fulton. He called me one of Elliot's women. And Jennifer. Jenn knows—about me and Elliot."

"What did he mean, one of Elliot's women," Barelli asked softly.

"I don't know." Finny caught back a sob. "I never knew there was anybody else."

She broke completely then and cried with abandon.

"Hush now, hush, Finny." He rocked her against his body. "It'll pass, it'll be all right."

"You were right," she choked through the tears. "I didn't ever think it through. I didn't want to."

He held her tightly. "What happened?"

She turned her cheek against his shoulder. "I took Jennifer home after we had dinner. Richard came barreling out of the house, and he called me a bitch and said never to come back again . . ." Finny was struggling to talk through the sobs that shook her. "Jenn was right there."

"Did she say anything?"

"No. She just watched, then Richard dragged her back into the house."

He held her and murmured to her until the storm of tears slowed. Finny began to relax under the hypnotic rhythm of his hand stroking up and down her spine. "I'm sorry," she whispered.

"What for?" His fingertips rotated slowly through the hair at the nape of her neck.

Her head dropped forward. "For dumping all this on you."

"Hush." His big hand traced the line of her cheek and stopped under her chin. He lifted her head slowly and brought his mouth down on hers.

Who would have guessed it could be so sweet? His lips moved lazily on hers and she relaxed into him. Her hands slid up his arms and across his shoulders to meet at the back of his neck. This was what she'd been wanting.

Barelli pulled out of the kiss slowly. Finny nestled against his shirt, comforted by the warmth of him, breathing in his scent.

It was sharp inside him, the wanting, pleasure edged by a need that had waited too long.

He reached across her to turn on the bedside lamp. Finny's eyes closed at the brightness.

"Open your eyes."

Finny looked up at him, into the depths of his dark eyes. Something in them made her heart beat slow and hard.

"I want you."

Finny nodded. "I want you, too."

Barelli's face hardened. "It's about the stupidest thing either one of us could do."

"I don't care." Finny's voice was low. "I need this—I need you, Barelli."

"Call me Chris, dammit." He pulled her hard against him.

CHAPTER

12

"How'd you ever get a name like Finny?" Barelli's deep voice interrupted Finny's slow descent into sleep.

The question hovered in her mind for a moment, its meaning clarifying slowly, like an image on developing film. "It's a nickname," she said finally.

Silence stretched through the room. "I'll bite, nickname for what?"

"Enfin." Finny yawned.

"What?"

"Enfin. It's a French word." She snuggled against the furry warmth of his arm and his hold tightened.

"Spell it."

She did.

"I've never heard that before. Your family French?"

Finny yawned again. "No. My mother's weird. When she was pregnant with me, she was afraid she'd lose herself in all the child care stuff. Oh—I can't stop yawning. Anyway, Mom signed up for a French class through some adult ed program."

"Okay, keep going."

"Aren't you tired?"

Barelli growled.

"All right, all right. Mom was in labor for a long time— fourteen, sixteen hours, I guess—and when I was finally born, my dad was so relieved that he told Mom she could name me."

"And she named you Enfin."

"Right."

Barelli waited for a minute, listening to her light breathing. "Finny," softly, "what does it mean?"

"At last."

"You're kidding."

Her hair tickled his chest as she shook her head.

"At last, huh?" Barelli chuckled. "At last Aletter."

"No jokes, Barelli. I've heard them all, and they're none of them funny."

"So how'd 'Enfin' become Finny?"

"Because everybody pronounced it the way it looks in English: in-fin. That evolved into Finny."

Barelli tucked her head under his chin. "You sure you aren't pulling my leg?"

Finny settled her backside against him. "I'm not but I will if it turns you on."

"I thought you were tired."

"I was."

"What woke you up?" His voice sank lower as she moved against him.

"The way you pronounced my name."

"I'm good at languages . . ." He nuzzled her neck.

"Mmmmm hmmmm."

Barelli was downstairs making coffee when the phone rang. He picked it up automatically. "Hello."

"That you, Chris?"

"Eddie?"

"Yeah."

The flat way he said it made Barelli clench up a little. "How'd you know to call me here?"

"It's the last number you left. Figured I'd try it when you weren't at home. We got a prelim on the Simons girl."

"And?"

"It was murder."

"Oh, shit," said Barelli under his breath. He had a picture in his mind of Finny, asleep upstairs, and the way her lips pursed sometimes when she took a breath, the little sound she'd made when he got out of bed. "What was the cause of death?"

"There was a mixture of barbiturates and booze in her stomach, but J.J. thinks she was smothered. It'll take a couple of days to get the lab work back, but he thinks whoever did it forced the killer cocktail down her after she was unconscious. He's checking out the sofa cushions."

"Set up to look like suicide." Barelli remembered Julia Simons's stark white face at the mortuary the day of Fulton's funeral. It hadn't looked all that different in death.

"Yeah. One other thing—she was about three months pregnant."

And the prize behind curtain three is. . . He sighed. "You got anything else?"

"No." Eddie paused. "You want me to call you at that number if I get something?"

It had been a long time since he'd heard Eddie be that polite. "No. I'm coming in pretty soon. Thanks."

"No problem." He hung up.

The coffee was still dripping into the carafe. He knew he shouldn't have gone to bed with her. What was the old line? Don't ever go to bed with anybody more screwed up than you are. Especially if people around her have a way of turning up dead.

"Goddammit." He liked Finny, wanted to know her better. If he hadn't been thinking with his balls, he'd have left last night. Now he'd have to put her through the drill, and she'd go back to hating his guts.

He paced around the kitchen. She'd done most of the work herself, she said. She was a feisty woman, smart and strong. Strong enough to push a pillow into Julia Simons's face until she couldn't breathe any more? Smart enough to bed down a cop to keep him from seeing her as a suspect? How much of what he was thinking came out of knowing he should never have touched her?

Barelli grabbed two mugs out of the cabinet and slammed them onto the counter top. He pulled the carafe off its burner and poured the coffee, ignoring the hissing of the brewing coffee dripping onto the hot plate. He shoved the carafe back and carried the cups out of the kitchen.

* * *

"Finny, wake up."

She burrowed deeper into the warmth under the blankets to get away from the voice that threatened her dream.

"Come on, I made you some coffee."

Finny pulled her pillow over her head.

"I mean it."

She yelped as the covers were pulled off the bed in one swift movement. "Hey!" She glared up at Barelli groggily.

He threw the covers on the foot of the bed. "There's a robe by your pillow. I need to talk to you."

Finny shivered in the cool morning air and sat up to tug the wine-red robe over her shoulders. "You don't snore, but you sure wake up mean," she grumbled. She pushed the pillows behind her back and pulled a blanket up under her arms. "Whatever happened to sweet nothings in the ear?"

He didn't answer, just took two mugs from the dresser behind him and handed one to her. When he sat on the bed, his unbuttoned shirt fell further open, framing the curling dark hair on his chest. He was freshly shaved and smelled of soap.

Finny wanted to pull him down and get creative, but not until she found out what was bothering him. Tradition had it that the woman was supposed to be the one to wake up nervous. "It's good coffee. Thanks."

"You're welcome."

Finny fought back a smile. He sounded like a kid standing on his dignity. How dignified could he be after what they'd done last night? "Listen, Chris, I—"

"I have to get to work pretty quick." Barelli's eyes met hers impersonally. "I wanted to go over a few things before I leave."

"Sure." She frowned into her cup. Maybe dignity wasn't the issue here.

"You said something last night about Richard Fulton— how he would have killed you if he could have." She looked up from her coffee, her eyes narrowing. "What kind of relationship did he have with his father?"

The coffee got hard to swallow. "Why are you asking?"

"Because I need to know."

"If the manuscript is behind Elliot's death, then Richard had nothing to do with it."

"Finny, I need to know."

"I told that to Chris, not Lieutenant Barelli."

"Don't be naive."

"Naive." She was careful putting the cup onto the night-stand. It would take too much time to clean up if she threw it at him. "I didn't know you had your badge on last night in bed."

Barelli had gotten off the bed and was rifling through his jacket pockets, frustration making him clumsy. Dammit, there wasn't any good way to do this. When he found his cigarettes, he lit one and exhaled the smoke as if he were re-leasing feelings. "I'm a cop, Finny, and I'm in the middle of a murder investigation. What you told me last night might have something to do with it."

She would be damned before she'd let out one atom of the tears pushing behind her eyes. "Congratulations," she said as she threw the blanket off her and got out of bed. "Your in-terrogation was very . . . satisfying."

"It wasn't like that and you know it."

"Bullshit. If it was anything else, then why the third de-gree now?" Her voice wavered, and she headed for the door.

"Lady, if this were a third degree, you'd know it. Ah, the

hell with it." Barelli grabbed her arm as she went by him. "Where were you Sunday night?"

"Let go of me." She wasn't at all sure how long she could keep from bursting into tears. "You damned jerk, let go of my arm."

Barelli shook her once. "Sunday night."

Her eyes blazed up at him. "At the Fultons' for the wake."

"What time did you get home?"

Finny stopped struggling. "Barelli, what are you doing?"

"What time?"

If it weren't so absurd, she'd be afraid. "I'm not sure, about eight-thirty, nine. I talked to Jenn for quite a while . . ."

"Did you see anybody, talk to anybody after you got home?"

She shook her head slowly, then stopped. "I called you, remember?"

Barelli's eyes widened a fraction, then resumed their usual half-mast position. "Yeah, but I wasn't there."

Finny jerked her shoulder from his hold.

"Was Julia Simons at the Fultons'?"

Finny stared up at him, rubbing the spot where he'd held her. "Yes, what of it?"

"Did you talk to her?"

"Yes."

His gaze dropped to his shirt, and he started buttoning it. "Julia Simons is dead."

"I know. She—"

His gaze flew up from his shirt. "You know?" He took one step toward her. "How?"

Finny backed up until she hit the side of the bed. "Tell me what's going on or get out of here."

"How do you know?"

"I heard yesterday." Finny swallowed against the dryness in her throat. "She killed herself."

Neither of them noticed the ash that dropped from Barelli's cigarette to the floor. "Who told you?"

Finny looked down at her hands. They were shaking.

"Dammit, Finny, don't fuck with me. Who told you?"

"Somebody at the office."

"Mrs. Leyden? Tell me, Finny."

"She called me yesterday, after you left here. One of Julia's friends found her and called the office while she was waiting for the police."

"We tried to keep it quiet." Barelli's voice was bitter. "So much for that."

Finny watched him in confusion. "What's all this about?"

"Julia Simons didn't kill herself. She was murdered."

Finny's breath went out in a short gasp, as if she'd been hit in the stomach.

Barelli nodded. "The office called this morning with the preliminary results from the autopsy."

"Oh, God," Finny whispered. She sat down on the bed.

"Are you sure nobody saw you that night?"

Finny's mind fixed on the incidentals. His scuffed shoes, wrinkled pants legs. She needed to go to the bathroom. She tilted her head back to look into his face. Hers was closed. "Thanks a lot, Barelli. First time I ever ended a one-night stand under suspicion of murder. I'm just sorry the victim was Julia."

"I have to check all the possibilities."

"And I was close at hand, right?"

Barelli tucked his shirt into his pants and reached for his tie. "She was pregnant."

"So what?"

Barelli watched her with hooded eyes. "Her lover was Elliot Fulton."

Finny shook her head sharply in a single negative motion.

"We have her diary, Finny. She had it all planned, how he would leave his wife and live with her in a cozy little place complete with a picket fence."

Finny stood up once more. "You think that I might have had a motive to kill her because of that, don't you? What? Jealousy, revenge? You haven't been right about one thing this morning, Barelli, but you sure were on target last night. It was the stupidest thing I ever did."

She walked around him and out the door.

Barelli was right behind her. Before she could get across the hall to her bedroom, he swung her around to face him.

"Get your hands off me."

"No." Barelli shook her. "The stupid thing was going to bed together *now*. Look, I—" He let his hands drop to his sides. "I didn't set you up last night. I'm a cop, that's all."

"Yeah, that's all."

He swore under his breath. "Look, I didn't want you to—"

"Get out. Either arrest me or get the hell out."

He turned away from her and walked down the hall. When he got to the stairs he looked back. "Don't go anywhere. Somebody from my office will be in touch."

"Can I go to work?" Finny shot back nastily.

Barelli just looked at her, his face bleak.

Finny swept into the bathroom and slammed the door.

CHAPTER

13

*F*inny's head was switching from bongos to snare drums by the time she walked through the portals of Lakin & Fulton. All had become clear to her as she'd searched for clothes to wear to work from the belongings thrown around her room. Number one: anger was a better emotion to focus on right now; going pale and wan over Barelli would be counterproductive. Number two: she wasn't going to wait around for someone to confess or get her off the hook. This was the eighties and no self-respecting Don Quixote would be caught dead tilting at her windmill. Too much commitment. The motto of the day was: You're on your own, kid.

She was late to work, not that it mattered, but Lisa Parmeter didn't know that. Her eyes glittered with the mean satisfaction that only the marginally useful employee can muster as she made a point of glancing at the brass sundial posing as a clock on one mauve wall.

Lisa wasn't overly endowed with brains, and her skills were minimal, but Finny had to concede the girl did have two things going for her—make that three. Two of them were packaged in the black sweater laminated to her body. The other was a supply of malice corrosive enough for her to hold her own among the acid-slingers at L&F.

Her own wasn't all she'd been holding if her funeral date with Greg was any indication. Maybe the first order of business should be finding out if Lisa knew what Greg had been doing last night. Barelli could speculate all he wanted about Leander Books, she'd start closer to home. It wasn't hard to imagine Greg throwing her possessions around just to get in his aerobics for the day.

Lisa flashed the smile she'd most likely learned from watching Miss America pageants. "Colter wants to see you right away. He was a little irritated that you didn't come in yesterday."

"Only a little irritated? That's a switch."

Lisa's lips closed over her teeth like a curtain between acts. "Greg had to cover for you, and he had more than enough of his own work to do."

"Don't tell me he had to stay late for once."

Lisa's glance sharpened. "No, he came with me to a lecture, but he had to rush to get out on time."

Greg at a lecture? The possibilities were limited. "Sowing Discord as a Leisure Activity?" "Sharpening Knives for Corporate Advancement?" "I'm sorry my being out affected your plans. What lecture was it?"

" 'Penny Stocks Will Rise Again.' It was out at the Merchandise Mart."

If that was true, at least Greg knew enough to stay in his

price range. "That must've been a long one. Such a complex topic and all."

"The time just seemed to fly." Lisa adjusted her smile rheostat back to full wattage. "Maybe I'll get my broker's license one of these days. Greg thinks I'd be a good one."

"I wouldn't be surprised, if you're willing to put in that extra time. After all, a—what was it, two-hour, three-hour?—lecture on top of a full day's work shows a lot of hustle."

Lisa sat a little straighter. "It was over three hours by the time the questions were over. We didn't even eat until ten."

Finny smiled absently. If it had happened, that let Greg out. Lisa, too. She mustn't underestimate dear little Lisa. It would help if she could verify that they'd been at the lecture. She'd gotten home by about nine or so, right in the middle of Pennies for Profit. "Was anybody else from the office there?"

"No." Lisa's eyes met hers earnestly. "You'd think more of the staff would've gone. I mean, it was a real chance to enhance our skills."

Finny was trying to figure out how she could prove they'd been at Pennies from Heaven. "I'd better get to work. Any messages?"

Lisa pulled pink squares of paper from the gray file on her desk, fanning them like playing cards. Three were Finny's, and she read them as she went back to the offices. The one from a would-be broker who worked down the street she crumpled and shoved into her coat pocket. The two clients she would call.

The muted clicking of computer keys and modulated conversations drifted over the secretarial area. She skirted round the edges to get to her office.

"Finny."

Jon Darrow stood in the doorway of his office. "Come in a minute. I need to talk to you."

What lucky star was she under today? "I was out yesterday, Jon. I have to get caught up."

"It can wait a minute. Come on in."

The days had worn badly on Jon. He was unkempt, tie loosened, top shirt button undone. His cuffs were grimy, as if he'd worn the pale blue shirt more than once. Finny had never before seen him with his shoes unshined. Something—desperation? grief?—had carved at the good-time padding of his face like a butcher trimming meat.

"Have you been sick, Jon?" He didn't move aside for her as she came through the door, forcing her to brush against him. He smelled stale and scared.

He pushed the door shut and shambled around his desk. His chair groaned under him as he sat down. "Have a seat."

She perched on the edge of the gray vinyl chair in front of his desk and set her handbag on the floor beside her.

"We need to talk business, Finny." Jon's bloodshot eyes met hers across his desk.

"Shoot."

Like any salesman, Jon sold himself before his product, but Finny had never seen anything she'd ever be interested in buying. The sports-world version of a country squire held no appeal for her. Today, even that had failed Jon. He rubbed one hand across his mouth, as though clearing it off, and she could see what a struggle it was for him to slip into his old groove.

"This thing about you and Elliot." He paused, hands trembling as he laced his fingers together on the desk top. His nails were bitten to the quick.

Finny stood up. "You mentioned that at the funeral the other day. I appreciate your concern, but its a dead issue." She winced at the way she'd put it, but Jon didn't notice.

He was back on his feet, too, as if he'd stop her if she tried to leave. "You don't understand. There's always been talk, but now it's getting to the point where it could be dangerous."

"What do you mean, dangerous?"

"You're up for the next vice-presidency, Finny. We all know that."

"Including Colter, I suppose."

Jon's gaze sidestepped hers. "You're too valuable to let go, and you've worked too hard to be passed over. If nothing happens to stop it, you'll get the VP."

He certainly had that worked out. "So?"

Jon relaxed a little and sat down again. "So, if Colter finds out about you and Elliot, nothing on God's green earth will make him promote you."

"And you want to help me."

His paste-on smile stretched into a poor imitation of his old salesman beam. "And I *can* help you."

"How's that, Jon?"

"I can make sure that it stays buried."

Finny resumed her seat. If this was what she thought it was. . . . "Now why would you want to do that for me?"

Jon leaned forward a little in his eagerness and held forth on how he and Finny could keep L&F on the track Elliot would have wanted, especially if she were a vice-president.

"And for the greater good of the company, you'd be willing to scotch any rumors that might derail my career, have I got that right?"

Jon nodded. "Of course, there would be some expenses involved."

"How much?"

"Twenty-five thousand." His presentation complete, Jon tilted back in his chair, trying to look confident that she'd see it his way. The light sheen of sweat on his face gave lie to the pose.

It was his struggle to pretend that all of this was legitimate that had Finny's stomach churning. She could understand his threatening her, or coming on like a sleazeball, but this sales pitch to her logic was unnerving. "That's a little steep, don't you think?"

Jon shrugged. "It's your career we're talking about." His meaty face slid into sullenness. "Besides, you know you can afford it."

Finny stared at him. He sounded sure and at the same time resentful about it. "What the hell gave you that idea?"

"Oh, come on, Finny. No extra income lately, no . . . prospects?"

It took her a minute, and even then she wasn't sure. Not the manuscript. Not him, too. "What are you talking about?"

Jon shook his head, disappointed. "Don't try to kid a kidder, Finny. I just want—" His telephone buzzed, and he answered it. "Yes?" He slid his hand over the speaker, eyes trained on Finny. "Wait a minute," he said. "Sure, Colter," he said back into the phone, "I'll get right on that. What? Yeah, she's right here. Okay."

Jon replaced the receiver. "Colter wants to see you in his office."

Finny got up from her chair.

"Finny." Jon stood up and came around his desk. "I know how close you and Elliot were. I won't talk, but you've got to pay retail for it."

"I don't have that kind of money, and I don't understand why you're doing this."

Jon moved closer to her. "I could tell you about Jon Junior's brush with the law, or how the college expenses for Deirdre are eating me alive. But I won't. Let's just say I need the money. Since you're into playing dumb, I'll throw in a little extra incentive: you pay me, and I'll promise not to let the cops know about you and Elliot."

Finny backed up to the door.

"You think they wouldn't be interested in knowing you balled him? You'd look awfully damned good as a murder suspect, wouldn't you? Killing him because he'd dumped you for somebody else."

She reached behind her for the doorknob that was digging into her back and turned it. "You don't have any kind of proof for that, Jon, and you know it."

"They can find their own proof. All they need is to be pointed in the right direction, by yours truly." He looked into her face, his smile growing as he took in the fear in her eyes. "You think about it, Finny, but think fast. The rate of inflation in this kind of thing can be pretty fierce."

To open the door, she had to move toward Jon. He backed up enough to let her get out, but no more than that, enjoying the way she shrank back to minimize their contact.

"I'll be in touch, Finny."

She pushed the door shut gently. Let him think he had her cowed, right up until she nailed his hide to a wall. Her anger grew with each step she took toward Colter's office. She banged on his door with her fist.

* * *

When she came out of Colter's office a half hour later, Finny felt like a loaded gun waiting to go off. If she had anything to say about it, it wouldn't be long until she did.

Colter had dropped the other shoe at last. As soon as the formalities of the audit were completed, she was officially unemployed. He had thrown in a generous severance settlement, the brocade vest across his paunch expanding with the thought of his own munificence. "You're a talented lady, Finny, but you an' I haven't ever pulled good in harness. With Elliot gone, I think you'd be happier somewhere else."

It had nearly choked her to be nice about it, but she'd done it. There was still too much to find out for her to vent her spleen now. But when this was all over . . .

Elaine was sitting at Finny's desk. Finny came into the office and threw her coat and purse onto the extra chair. "What are you doing here?"

"Hiding out." Her shrewd eyes took measure of Finny. "You look like you just got rolled. What's up?"

Finny laughed shortly. "You're not far off. So far this morning I've sat through a blackmail attempt and the termination of my services. Got any aspirin?"

"Blackmail? Colter fired you? What the hell—"

"Don't freak out." Finny pulled the chair closer to the desk and dumped her stuff on the floor. When she'd sat, she tilted back in the chair and rested her heels on the desk. "I was going to quit anyway. I'd rather starve than work for Denver's answer to Ben Cartwright. Blackmail, now—that was a new experience."

"Who?"

"Jon Darrow."

Elaine's face sagged. "It figures. What's his problem? Into the dealers too heavy?"

"Nope, gotta pay that tuition and all."

"Tuition, hell," Elaine scoffed. "It's coke."

Finny whistled soundlessly. "Very interesting. That might explain the ragged edges. He scared me." She met Elaine's eyes. "How do you know that—about the coke?"

Elaine's gaze dropped to the desk. "My son told me." Her mouth curved in a smile, but her eyes were desolate. "Apparently they've shared the same dealer."

Finny nodded.

"What'd he use as leverage—oops, shouldn't ask that, I guess."

Finny smiled wryly. "Old scandal. Elliot and I had a fling a long time ago."

The animated interest in Elaine's face stilled. "I have to admit I've wondered."

"You probably won't believe this, but there hasn't been anything more than friendship between us for nearly nine years."

Elaine smiled. "Why wouldn't I believe you?"

Finny sighed. "It makes too good a motive for murder, I guess, at least it does to Jon."

"What harm could it do you if anybody did know about you and Elliot?"

"He figures I'd never make VP if Colter knows. Little does he realize."

"The sleazy bastard. What the hell is happening around here?" Elaine exploded. "First Elliot, then Julia. Now this business with Jon. It's scary, Finny."

"I know. It's as if somebody pulled a loose string or something, and the whole place is unraveling."

The phone buzzed. "Oh, hell. What now?"

Elaine picked up the receiver. "Yes? Okay, I'll be there in a minute." She made a face as she hung up. "They tracked me down. Ardith couldn't format a report by herself if her life depended on it. I've got to get back."

"What drove you in here, anyway?"

"Gloria's been hanging crepe all morning, and I couldn't hack any more of it. She's just sick about Julia, and what can I do? I don't know why she even bothered to come in today." Elaine paused, her hand on the doorknob. "What are you going to do about Jon?"

"Tell the cops about him, I guess." Finny got up and hung her coat on the rack by the door. "What would you do?"

"That would depend on what kind of relationship I had with the cops." Her eyes held a warning. "At the very least, stay away from him." She made a point of locking the door before she pulled it shut behind her.

Stay away from Jon she would do. Calling the cops would require a little thought. Talking to Barelli again wasn't that appealing an idea. How much could it help her situation to tell him that somebody else thought she might have committed murder? He'd probably think it was some tortuously conceived double bluff.

Finny sat down behind her desk. Last week she thought she was having a mid-life crisis. This week she was minus a friend, had lost her job, and was a suspect in two different murders, although the ones doing the suspecting had her figured for only one each. Or had Barelli gone back to tying her into Elliot's murder, too, without telling her? No matter.

175

She had found out a few things. Either Greg hadn't searched her house, or Lisa was in it with him and was lying to cover for him. It was hard to imagine anyone capable of fluttering over Pitching for Pennies in the role of conspirator, but the possibility was there. The list of candidates for the role of killer was getting longer—Richard and Cronin were already featured players, and now the shadowy presence of Leander Books had to be taken into account as well. And then there was Colter . . .

Jon Darrow was leading the pack for a lot of reasons right now. If he was into drugs, who knows what he'd do? The way he'd been talking, he had to know about the manuscript. If she could be certain of that, it might tie him in to Elliot's death. It didn't take any effort for her to imagine Jon committing murder. Barelli might have been right, thinking the manuscript hadn't been in Elliot's possession when he was killed.

She already knew that Cronin was keeping his knowledge of the manuscript to himself. That might simply be caginess on his part, or it could indicate something more sinister.

She kept picking up threads, but they were all too short to lead anywhere. All she knew was, too many people thought they had threads leading to her, and it made her nervous. The only thing she could think to do was to keep looking. One of the threads had to lead her to a killer.

INTERLUDE

*D*enver's high rises glimmered in the background, as far away as childhood dreams. Two nearby bridges carried streams of cars, flowing over the wide, shallow river.

Larkspur slipped on the icy bike path that ran beside the water. The tattered pack he held close to his chest threatened to slide to the ground, and he clutched it so hard that the broken zipper on his stained parka dug into his skin.

It wasn't far now, his stash. Close enough to the tracks so he could get to it if he had to leave in a hurry. He chuckled. He was leavin' in a big hurry this time. His boots crunched across the gravel between the railroad tracks. The growling of the crane at the Eighth Avenue bridge drifted over the flats.

The old viaduct wasn't safe. They were rebuilding it, afraid one of those supports would fold up, kill somebody. Sure would make one hell of a boom if it did. He coughed, the breath rattling in his throat. He'd take all his stuff this time, when he got the papers Bennie found.

Larkspur stopped to catch his breath. Over in the yards, men were coupling an engine onto two more, probably for a coal train. He moved on, careful to keep the empty cars between him and the men.

When he got to the old bridge, he skirted round the gravel piled near the end support. The workers were down at the other end, the smoke from the growling crane drifting across the tracks between them. He kept one eye on them as he approached the second support.

He leaned against the grainy surface of the old concrete legs. His fingertips scrabbled for a hold on the edge of the crack that snaked from the middle of the support. A chunk of concrete, about eight inches wide, lifted out like a piece from a jigsaw puzzle, and behind it was the narrow cavity he'd hollowed out.

He'd had to roll up the papers to get them through the hole, but it hadn't hurt them, although the cardboard cover wouldn't roll, and he'd torn it off.

Larkspur heard the crunch of gravel from behind and turned sharply. Nothing there. He listened for other sounds beneath the machinery whine across the tracks, then turned back to his stash.

He pulled the papers out slowly. Didn't want to tear nothing. The boy promised him five thousand dollars for 'em in good shape, shook hands on it. Two pages slid from the bundle to the ground and he bent to pick them up. Words marched across the page in strong, angled script.

no more books on my account. Folks is big on followin' in other people's footsteps. To hear 'em talk, there ain't no better a person can do than go 'long behind them that's gone before. Always did seem to me that if that was how it *ought* to be, there wouldn't a been no white folks further west than Virginia, but then my Geography ain't—

Larkspur had a spider-crawl feeling between his shoulder blades, like somebody was watching him. He could have been followed. A glance around showed nothing. He smoothed the two loose pages onto the pile of papers and slid them carefully into his pack. He was getting out of Denver tonight.

CHAPTER

14

*T*he elevator hissed open at the second level of the parking garage, and Finny jockeyed the box she carried through the door. It hadn't taken long to clean out her desk. Beyond her files there was little more than an assortment of office supplies. The detritus of inkless pens and mismatched earrings were as evocative as driftwood, but not as useful.

It was over. She could come in tomorrow for whatever had escaped her notice today. Greg was calling her clients to introduce himself. She had to decide whether to issue a sleaze alert to them about him. For now, she was hungry, and what she wanted were flautas at Joe's Buffet. Everything else could go to hell.

The concrete walls echoed back the sharp click of her heels as she walked toward L&F's parking area. Before she could cross the access lane, a brown Mercedes jerked around a support column and flashed by her. The driver was Marian Fulton and, if her expression was anything to go by, she was furiously angry.

Finny stared after her. Colter had said something about seeing Marian today when he had eased her out of his office this morning. They must have had some session. Colter and Elliot had worked out their own style of getting along, but Marian and Colter were a whole new ballgame.

Before Finny could walk on, a hand pulled at her shoulder. Jon Darrow, Finny thought, and dropped the box, spinning around, her hand already clamping into a fist around her keys for extra hitting power, cursing herself for not getting a security guard to come with her. She managed to stop her hand before it thudded into Bart Cronin's face.

"Jesus Christ," she said and slumped against the side of a car. Another car down the row coughed into life and snarled for the exit, its transmission squealing like a frightened pig.

Cronin dropped the arm he'd brought up to protect his face. "What the hell was that all about?" He had the nerve to sound irritated.

"I thought you were somebody else. What are you doing creeping around here?"

"I was on my way up to your office."

"Why?"

Cronin glanced around the concrete box. "I need to talk—you want to get out of here, maybe have a drink?"

Finny knelt and started picking up the jumble of items that had fallen from the box. Pens, a compact, a pack of tissues, extra paper. "I don't think so. I've got a lot to do this afternoon." She fumbled with a box of paper clips, and Cronin went down on one knee to help her with the rest. They finished together, and Finny hefted the box. "Maybe some other time." Maybe never. Cronin had lied to her, and he was after the manuscript. Maybe he was the one who searched her house last night.

Shouldn't have thought of that now. The low ceiling seemed to press even lower, and she couldn't hear anybody else on this level. She and Cronin were alone. "I've got to go now." She was dismayed at the waver in her voice.

Cronin's eyes narrowed. "What's the matter?"

Finny fumbled with her keys and unlocked her car door. She slid behind the wheel, put the box behind her in the back seat, and pulled the door toward her. Cronin grabbed it by the edge of the window. "Wait a minute. I'm sorry I scared you. I need to talk to you, and since I was downtown, I figured I'd come up to your office instead of calling ahead. It's important, Finny." The scoutmaster look was back again.

"Get in." She watched him in the rearview mirror as he came around to the passenger side. He wanted something and wanted it bad, but it couldn't be half as much as she wanted to know about where he fit into things.

Finny started the engine as he got into the car. "I was just going for Mexican food. All right?"

"Can I get something to drink?"

"Sure."

"Then it's okay with me."

As she drove out of the parking garage, Cronin glanced at the box in the back seat. "I hope we got everything. We should've looked under the cars."

"Doesn't matter." Finny flashed her parking pass at the lot attendant and looked for an opening in the traffic. "It's just the junk I never threw out of my desk drawers. Nothing valuable."

"And today was cleaning day?"

"Today was the day I got my walking papers." She pulled out into the stream of cars on Stout Street.

Cronin shot her a look of surprise.

Joe's Buffet had been an institution on Santa Fe Drive for as long as Finny had been in Denver. Its edges had been smoothed the last few years with new fixtures and cosmetic updating, but the food hadn't changed. People still came from all over town for the Mexican hamburgers, and Finny still came for the flautas.

Cronin played it safe with an order of tacos.

"So tell me what you wanted to talk about." Finny sipped her beer. She'd waited through the drive over here, and Cronin still hadn't come to the point.

"I was hoping you could help me out with something."

"What is it?"

"Elliot bought something the day he died, something very valuable, and it may have had something to do with his murder." He recounted the business of the manuscript, basically what she'd heard him say to Marian, but this time he went the rest of the way. "If what I've heard is true, and I think it is, the manuscript is by Mark Twain, previously unpublished, incredibly valuable."

"I should think so. How did Elliot get hold of it?"

Cronin lit a cigarette. "Elliot was convinced that not everything Twain wrote was published. And there was good reason to think so. After Twain's wife and daughters died, the things he wrote were scathing and took such a bleak view of mankind that he arranged to suppress their publication until well after his death. Some of them were printed for the first time fairly recently."

"Here you go, honey. Your plate is hot." The waitress slid

Finny's platter of flautas in front of her and presented Cronin with his tacos. "You want something else from the bar?"

"Another round." Cronin mashed out his cigarette and pulled his plate closer. "For a long time nobody knew what had been suppressed, then *Letters from the Earth* came out in the sixties, and there was an edition of *The Mysterious Stranger* compiled after his death." He took a large bite of one taco.

Finny had finished one flauta and was beginning the next.

"As you can guess, there've been rumors for years about other works, and nowhere were they stronger than on the collection circuit. Elliot believed them, and he put the word out a long time ago that he was interested in anything by Twain, so I'm sure that's how he heard about this one."

"I'm surprised I didn't see anything about it in the papers," Finny said. "You'd think that an unknown Twain would cause an enormous uproar."

Cronin's eyes met hers. "Come on, Finny. Surely you realize it was stolen. I don't know how Elliot got hold of it, but I can guarantee you that whoever sold it to him either stole it or got it from someone who did."

"Sounds like trying to establish provenance in stock ownership. Are you sure this Twain manuscript even exists?"

"I know it does," Cronin said grimly. "It was taken to one of the shadier 'experts' in the field to be authenticated." Cronin used a fork on the lettuce and cheese that had dropped from his tacos. "He was excited enough to let the word out after he'd seen the thing."

"Didn't he leak who had brought it to him?"

"No way. He was cautious to the point of fear about letting that get around. That's what fits in with Elliot's death. This is one of the hottest finds ever. You can bet that whatever collectors have heard about it are tripping over themselves and each other to get to that manuscript." His smile was bleak. "And some of them wouldn't have stopped at murder, if that's what it took."

Finny suppressed a shiver. "But how could Elliot have paid for it? It must be worth a fortune."

"I don't know how Elliot got it. I wish I did. I do know that it was stolen from whoever found it first or it would be talked about in banner headlines to hype the bidding. The only reason to sell it on the black market is because it's hot."

Barelli had called it big time. Finny thought of the chaos in her house and her ripped nightgown. Maybe his concentration on Leander Books wasn't so far off base.

"What's the matter?" Cronin asked.

Finny met his pale gray eyes and imagined they had cross hairs behind them. Just talking about the manuscript had charged his batteries. How much of what he'd said did she dare believe?

"You have it, don't you?" Cronin whispered.

Finny's eyes widened. "No, I don't!" The family at the table next to theirs glanced over at her. "I don't know anything about it," she said more quietly. "Nothing beyond what you've told me."

Cronin's mouth tightened impatiently. "I hope you don't plan on anybody's believing that." He lit another cigarette. "How do you plan to live now that you're out of work?"

"What business is it of yours?"

"You were close to Elliot, you just happen to have left your job—" He held up one hand. "I don't care if you were fired or not. Anybody who's after the manuscript is going to be looking for the logical person to have it. And here you are."

"And so are you." Finny stood up. "Are you the one who searched my house last night?"

Cronin's cynical smile died. "Searched your house? Are you joking?"

"Some joke. If I'm the logical person to have the manuscript, then you're the logical one to be looking for it." To the point of killing Elliot for it?

Cronin's lips curved in a small, secret smile. "I didn't search your house, Finny. I could hazard some guesses as to who might have, though."

"You can hazard them to the police. I'm sure they'll be in touch when I've told them what you said."

Cronin shrugged. "I'm always happy to cooperate with the authorities."

Finny dug through her purse and pulled out a ten-dollar bill. "You'll have to get a ride back. I'm not in the mood for company."

Cronin's eyes narrowed. "Take care of the manuscript," he said softly.

A file folder landed in the middle of Barelli's desk. He glanced up at Eddie Apodaca. "What's that?"

"The autopsy results on Julia Simons."

Barelli looked back at the file without enthusiasm. "J.J. didn't waste any time."

"When has he ever?" Eddie leaned one hip against the edge of the desk. In his beige corduroy suit, he looked more like a teacher than a cop, slight and neat, his short black hair closely trimmed.

"Where'd you get the tie?" The red plaid over a lavender background wasn't Eddie's style.

Apodaca glanced down at it. "Tanya's birthday present. Can I talk to you a minute?"

"Why not?" Barelli leaned back in his chair and got a cigarette and matches out of his shirt pocket.

"I was thinking about this morning."

Barelli blew out the match. "So?"

"You logged in the Aletter woman's phone number last night and never called back in to change it."

Barelli frowned at the burning tip of his cigarette.

"You got on the same clothes you wore yesterday."

Barelli glanced up at the hint of question in Eddie's voice. "You want to get to the point?"

"You know what the point is." Eddie looked around the partitions that honeycombed the Homicide department. "What the fuck are you doing?"

Barelli sat up in his chair. "Who're you? The world's first black Chicano Jewish mother?" He started to get up.

The wiry brown hand on his shoulder changed his mind. "Unh-unh, Chris. You been duckin' out, won't even talk to me."

"So I don't feel like talking." Barelli ground out his cigarette in the overflowing ashtray on his desk. "Why don't you lay off?"

"Because you are fucking yourself, and I don't feel like watching."

"Don't watch," Barelli said viciously. His words hung in the silence between them. Barelli glanced up at Apodaca's face, then back down at his desk. "Shit, Eddie."

The tightness went out of Apodaca's face. "What do you hear from Monica?"

"The child support's not enough, Tracy needs braces." He lit another cigarette. "She's still shacked up with that lawyer—what's his name."

"The same one—"

"The one she left me for. Yeah."

"Kids tell you?"

"Yeah."

"Talk to me, man."

Barelli shifted uncomfortably in his swivel chair. "What do you want, Eddie, details? I know what I did was stupid—"

"Stupid? It's suicide! Not only could you get your ass kicked out here, you could be brought up on charges."

"Eddie, I'm quitting. I only got a month to go. I know she didn't have anything to do with the Fulton killing."

Eddie's hand slapped down hard on the desk top. "How long we been together, eleven years? You been talkin' about quittin' for five of 'em. And you don't mean it, man. You never have meant it for real. This time you gonna be out before you get your head straight." He levered himself off the desk. "It'll be too late, Chris."

"She's okay, Eddie," Barelli said in a low voice. "I like her."

Apodaca frowned down at him. "This ain't just dumb, Chris. It's wrong."

"You think I don't know that?"

"Then why you doin' it?"

"I've got to have something for me."

CHAPTER

15

*W*hen all else fails, clean.

Finny had spent the afternoon picking up the mess her intruder had made the night before. With every item she put back in its place, every piece of broken glass thrown out, each garment replaced, she tried to put together the pieces of the puzzle. For her pains she got a return engagement of her headache and a fairly clean house.

Finny was bringing the final load of trash out to the garbage cans beside the fence when she saw the old woman. Shuffling in her peculiar side-to-side gait, she came up the alley. Something in the way her heavy body moved kept Finny there watching her. As she came closer, Finny could see that tears had tracked down her pasty cheeks.

Her shoulders were shaking with the sobs that came between her words, said over and over. "He's dead. Oh, God, he's dead. He's dead." The cracked voice had a keening sound to it that raised the hairs on the back of Finny's neck.

"Oh, God, he's—"

Finny couldn't stand the sound. "What's the matter? Do you need help?"

There was nothing but grief in the old woman's eyes. "Bennie's dead, my Bennie's dead."

"I'm sorry." Finny patted at her shoulder. "Was he related to you?"

The old woman drew the back of her hand under her nose. "We was together. Me and him was goin' to make a new start."

A new start, Finny thought. In her food-stained gray coat and pink flowered housedress, holes in the cotton hose that bagged over her swollen ankles.

What should she do? She couldn't leave her here, crying in the alley. "Where do you live?"

The old woman's eyes, aswim in tears, looked up the alley. "At the house."

"Is it far?" Finny asked. "It's getting colder. You don't want to get sick, now, do you?" She put a hand at the woman's back and gently urged her in the direction she'd pointed. The old woman's worn shoes shuffled against the asphalt.

They went up the middle of the alley. The garbage trucks had yet to come through: a forest of dented metal cans, some overturned by dogs or ragpickers, overflowed with trash. Backyards lapped up to the edges of the alleys, hemmed in by their fences.

"How far is it?" Finny asked as they came to the end of the alley.

"Not far." The old woman began her keening again. "He's dead. I ain't never gonna see him again."

Glass wind chimes sounded an alarm from a balcony of the high rise they were passing, the bits of glass tossing in the rising wind. "What happened?"

"Bennie run out in the street, got hit by a car." She shook her head back and forth. "Hit by a car."

"I'm so sorry." Finny shivered, wishing she'd worn her coat. "Where is this place you live?"

"He was runnin'. Run right across Speer into traffic. Somebody was lookin' for him. Lord Jesus, he just run right out."

Finny was listening, but her mind's eye was projecting a picture she didn't want to see. She'd left her keys lying on the kitchen counter, and the back door was unlocked. Had she closed the back gate?

"—layin' in the street callin' for Larkspur." The old woman's grief was raw, out of the heart of her. "Louis saw; he told me."

A child squatting behind the chain-link fence around his apartment house watched curiously as they went by, his unembarrassed stare following them like a portrait's eyes.

Back and forth, back and forth, her heavy body followed the cracked and broken flagstone sidewalk to the street.

Come on, lady. Finny had to get back to her house. What if the intruder came back?

"He was out of his head, callin' for Larkspur. 'Larkspur,' he says, 'the huckleberries is dead.' Over and over, Louis said, callin' to Larkspur about the huckleberries." She wiped her nose with the back of her hand. "I wasn't there. I didn't get to say no good-byes."

"Wait a minute." Finny grabbed the old lady's shoulder as they came to an intersection. "Let the cars go past." When the way was clear, Finny asked her which way they should go.

The old lady stepped off the curb and started across the street. Finny walked behind her, in a frenzy of impatience to deliver her and get back to her house. She sighed in relief as the woman went up the steps of the house on the corner, an old Denver square, its porch sagging like elderly flesh.

It was one of the neighborhood rest homes scattered throughout Capitol Hill, halfway houses for the chronically mentally ill dumped during the 'liberation' of the state hospitals during the sixties.

Two men, one heavy and flabby, one beanpole thin, flanked the sharp-chinned woman who pointed at them from the porch. "Hey, Leila," she called, malice in her voice, "we had chocolate cake at lunch."

The heavy man got to his feet and yelled into the open doorway. "Sarah Jane, Leila's back!"

Leila paid no mind to either of them, shuffling across the porch and through the door. Her shoulder brushed against the edge of the doorjamb, dislodging flakes of dirty white paint.

Finny followed her into the entryway. The smell of old meals struggled to overcome the haze of disinfectant in the air. A grimy fluorescent light fixture dimly lit the area, barely reflecting off the red and white Coke machine that loomed against one wall.

A blonde woman in faded jeans and a plaid shirt came quickly around the corner. "Leila, there you are! We've been looking for you."

She might as well have been talking to the Coke machine. Leila shuffled toward the stairs that zigzagged up to the second floor.

The woman turned to Finny. "She just wanders off sometimes. Where did you find her?" Hollywood would have cast her as a nun, scrub-faced and clear-eyed. The camera would have had to skip over the nicotine stains on her blunt fingers.

"She was in the alley beside my house, about three blocks from here," Finny said. "She was so upset that I wanted to make sure she got home okay."

The other woman darted a quick look up the stairs. "She had a friend who was killed last night. A traffic accident."

Finny was already edging toward the door. "She told me. Listen, I need to get back to my place. I hope she'll be all right." She went out to the porch.

"Thanks for helping her," the woman called.

"No problem." Finny ran down the steps to the sidewalk. "It's getting cold," she heard the woman say to the people on the porch. "Don't you want to come in?"

She retraced her steps quickly. The neighborhood was quiet this time of day, kids home from school and watching cartoons, dinners being thought about, a few joggers beating the evening rush.

She strode down the quiet alley, glancing from left to right, on the alert for unusual movement. Her back gate to the alley was partly open, as she'd left it. Finny slowed down as she went up the steps to the back porch. Through the weather-stained windows she surveyed the area. The doorknob turned easily in her hand, and she pushed the door open. She crossed to the kitchen door and opened it, looking into the room. Nothing different.

Finny started across the threshold, then stopped and, feeling like a fool, peered through the crack between the wall and the door. How many times in movies and TV shows had the good guy walked blithely into a room while the bad guy hid behind the door?

No one was there.

Finny closed the back door behind her and leaned against it. Her eyes focused on the red light of the coffee maker as she consciously slowed her breathing to listen to the silent air in the room. It felt normal. There was no frisson of awareness that something indefinable had changed. She crossed to the counter and closed her fingers over the keys that lay near the coffee maker. Their serrated edges pressed into her skin.

She walked quietly into the dining room and again stood still to assess the quality of the air. Dust motes voyaged lazily in the sunbeams thrusting through the shutters over the living room windows. Everything looked the same, the cushions back on the sofa, the books replaced on their shelves. The house was silent.

Finny walked through the living room to the stairs, the floorboards creaking sporadically as she crossed the room. She hesitated at the foot of the stairs, took one step, then another. Her ears strained for sounds overhead.

She was at the first landing, just turning to go up the rest of the stairs when she heard the tapping sound below. She froze, heart pounding. Before she could move, the sound came again. Then the soft chimes of the doorbell rang.

Finny sagged against the banister. Just someone at the door. She walked down the stairs on shaking legs.

It was Barelli. "Go away."

When his knocking had progressed to banging on the oval window, she opened the door a crack. "Get lost."

"Goddammit, Finny," Barelli growled, "cut it out." He

shoved hard on the door and, when Finny fell back, surged through and slammed it shut behind him. "I need to talk to you."

In the face of his anger, her own wilted. She turned away from him. "You scared me half to death. Why did you tap on the door like that?"

"I saw you through the window." He pulled off his overcoat and hung it on the coat tree. "I was tapping to get your attention." He stepped closer to her, puzzled at the fear on her face. "Why should that scare you?"

Finny cupped her elbows in her hands, then rubbed one arm. "I thought somebody might have gotten into the house while I was outside. I was checking to make sure."

"Are you out of your mind? After what happened last night? Why didn't you call the cops?"

"After what happened this morning, I'm not too thrilled with cops." She walked away from him into the kitchen.

Barelli followed her through the swinging door. "I want to talk to you about that."

Finny didn't look at him. She got her coffee mug off the kitchen table and carried it over to the coffee maker on the counter. "Why? I didn't think you'd come back here unless it was to arrest me." She turned her back on him as she poured the coffee into her cup. "Or is that why you're here?"

"No, that's not why I'm here." Barelli came up behind her. "Can I have some of that?"

"You know where the cups are." Finny took her coffee to the table and sat down.

Barelli filled his cup and came over to sit across the table from her. "Finny, I wanted to—I've been thinking—dammit." He slammed the mug onto the table. Coffee splashed out onto his hand, and he covered it with his other hand. "It's not easy for me to talk to you."

"Tough." Finny resisted the urge to get a cool cloth for his hand. Let him deal with his problems.

"You never let me finish this morning." His eyes stayed on his hands. "I don't think you killed Julia Simons."

Finny's eyes shimmered with tears. "Gee, thanks, Barelli. That makes me feel a lot better."

He reached across the table and picked up her hand in his. "It was Chris last night, Finny. We did get that far."

Finny pulled away from him. "It's not that easy. You made me feel like shit this morning, Barelli. You hid behind your badge and let me twist in the breeze." She held the cup tightly between both hands. "Why did you come here?"

Barelli stood up and walked toward the window. "I haven't been worth shooting all day," he said to the glass. "I keep thinking about last night." The face he turned toward her had the same confusion on it she could feel inside herself. "Dammit, it *meant* something to me, Finny."

She should tell him to get lost—but she knew she wasn't going to. She also wasn't going to think about what she was getting herself into. "I'm hungry. You want something?"

"Sure."

"I've been cleaning up the mess our unknown friend made." Finny squatted to look into the lower shelves of the refrigerator. "You like ham? No, wait, how about BLTs?"

"Fine, whatever." Barelli came over to her. His broad fingers closed around one arm, and he pulled her to her feet, pushing the refrigerator door shut. "I don't want to just leave it at that, Finny. The quick gloss-over and on to the next topic. I know I hurt you this morning, and I don't want you to pretend it didn't happen."

She was tired of battling with herself, tired of the fear that had become a constant companion since Elliot's death. "God, I wish I could trust you," Finny whispered. She wiped angrily at the tears that brimmed in her eyes.

Barelli put his arms around her and held her close to him. "We got off to a bad start, Finny. You can trust me."

Finny laughed a little wildly as she pulled out of his hold. "Right. Sure I can—"

"Stop it, Finny!" Barelli pulled her back against him. "Listen to me," low-voiced. "I panicked this morning. I'm so far out on a limb over this, I've got birds in my hair."

Finny swallowed painfully. "Damn it all, I feel like all I do anymore is cry."

Barelli cupped her chin in one big hand. "Finny, you've been through a lot. Murder has a ripple effect. It changes everybody who comes into contact with it. Give yourself a little time."

"Chris." Finny paused until she could control her voice. "I didn't have anything to do with Julia's death."

"I know that. I knew it this morning." He pulled her closer and rested his chin on her hair. "I told you—I panicked. I'm just as scared as you are, Finny. Maybe more."

"Why?"

"Because you get to me. I've been making the wrong decisions because of you. We should never have slept together, at least not until this case is over. I knew that, and I stayed with you anyway."

Finny drew far enough away from him to look up into his face. "I'm sorry."

"I'm not." He kissed her. "We strike sparks off each other." His hands stroked down her back and lingered at her hips. "You make me feel alive again."

197

Finny let her hand drop back and met Barelli's eyes. "Come to bed with me."

They held each other's hands tightly as they went up the stairs.

"You've just won the man of the day award."

"Only the day?"

"You wouldn't believe the competition." Finny traced the scar across Barelli's hip. The raised, white tissue extended from his pelvic bone down the side of his leg. "What happened here?"

"Land mine in 'Nam." His lips explored the hollow over her throat. "You smell good."

Finny arched against him as his lips neared her breast. "I should smell like sweat. I've been running up and down the stairs all afternoon."

"Your sweat smells good."

Finny's stomach growled loudly. "Oops."

Barelli propped himself up on his elbows and smiled down at her. "Didn't you eat any lunch?"

"With a man, yet." His eyes seemed bottomless, clear brown wells. How did they close themselves off so completely when he was angry? The fringe of lashes was black against his olive skin. "Why do men always have the thickest lashes? It isn't fair."

"Who said things should be fair?" He leaned his forehead against hers. "What man?"

"Bart Cronin," Finny said reluctantly. She didn't want to think about the real world yet.

"That's the competition?"

Finny shifted her head to nip his ear. "You're conceited, Lieutenant."

Barelli's lips skimmed across her cheek. "No, I'm not." His breath tickled against her skin.

She heard the uncertainty in his voice and pushed at his shoulders. "The only thing he was interested in was the manuscript. He's sure I have it."

Barelli surveyed her thoughtfully. "And how did he get that idea?"

Finny sat up and put her feet onto the floor. "If you want to hear any more, you'll have to come downstairs. I'm famished."

"What time is it?"

"Four-thirty." Finny pulled on her robe.

"You look like a courtesan in that." Barelli's long fingers slid over the thick ruby velvet. His hand clenched the lapel and he pulled her close for a kiss.

Finny pulled away. "Food, Barelli. If you want a return on your investments, you have to shelter your income."

"Huh?"

"Old financial world proverb."

"God, you're poetic." Barelli let her up. "I've got to go back to the office pretty soon. To check in again with Berkeley about Leander Books, among other things," he answered the questioning look on her face.

"I'll fix you a sandwich," Finny said. "Get dressed."

The smoky sweet scent of bacon greeted Barelli as he came into the kitchen. He was suddenly ravenous. He snitched a piece of bacon off the folded paper towels where they were draining.

"Leave some for the sandwiches," Finny said automatically, and Barelli had a swift, sharp sense of homecoming.

"Tell me about Cronin," was all he said. His even teeth crunched the crisp bacon.

Finny shrugged. She spread mayonnaise over the slices of bread lined up in front of her. "How many of these can you eat?"

"Two."

"Okay." She gathered the rest of the ingredients.

"I ran into him in the parking lot at L&F." The crisp snick, snick of torn lettuce punctuated her words as she told him about the lunch.

"He made me nervous, but after dealing with Jon and Colter earlier, Cronin was a piece of cake."

"What do you mean?"

"Jon tried to blackmail me—he thinks I killed Elliot—and Colter fired me. It's been a swell day." Finny put the completed sandwiches onto plates and carried them to the table.

"Blackmail?"

"I'll tell you while we eat. Get some milk out of the fridge, will you?"

"You definitely tend to bring out the best in people," Barelli said after she'd told him about Jon Darrow. "I'll nose around, see if there's anything to the drug stuff. You steer clear of that guy."

"I plan to. He scared me."

The telephone rang. It was for Barelli.

"I have to go," he said as he hung up the receiver.

"Back to the real world."

Barelli seemed to hear what she was thinking. "It's not going to change, Finny. Trust me, please."

Finny put her palm against his cheek. "Everything's happened so quickly."

He turned his mouth into her palm and kissed it lingeringly. "Trust me."

"I want the manuscript." The hoarse whisper rasped over the phone. "I know you've got it."

Finny's hand tightened on the receiver. "What are you talking about? Who is—"

"I want *The Death of Huckleberry Finn.* If I don't get it, it'll be the death of *you.*"

"I don't have it!" The phone clicked, and Finny was listening to the hum of the empty line.

She slammed down the receiver. "I don't have the goddamned manuscript!" The house answered with silence.

The living room was in shadow, the windows edged with the last efforts of the setting sun. Finny groped for her watch on the coffee table. She must have slept over an hour. The book that had slid off her chest when she answered the telephone thudded onto the floor. She put it on the table and got up to turn on a light.

Check the doors, she thought, and then, heart racing, she hastened to the back window where last night's visitor had come in. The plywood was still in place.

It was so quiet. Finny turned on the radio in the kitchen, then turned it off. She couldn't hear if anybody tried to get in. At the thought, she was dialing the number Barelli had given her.

He wasn't there. Finny swallowed the lump in her throat. "Tell him I received a threatening phone call," she told the woman in Homicide. "It was about the manuscript. He'll know what that means. Tell him I'm all right, but I need to talk to him. Thank you."

She would make some coffee, and Chris would call soon. She was perfectly safe.

Finny was scooping coffee into the filter basket when it occurred to her that her anonymous caller had given her the name of the manuscript. *The Death of Huckleberry Finn*. Funny, neither Cronin nor Barelli had ever told her. Lord, if that was really it, no wonder people were scrambling to find it. Beyond the money . . . just to read it would be an incredible experience. That explained the entry on Elliot's calendar: Finn. Not a shadowy extension of Leander Books after all. Elliot must have been delirious with excitement when he got his hands on that manuscript.

She filled the coffee maker with water and turned it on. What was teasing at her mind? Something familiar, something she should remember. Had Elliot mentioned the Twain book, something she'd forgotten in all that had happened since?

Finny moved restlessly around the kitchen, her surface thoughts cluttered with details. If Chris spent the night, did she have anything for breakfast? She could run over to King Soopers and pick up something at the bakery. Croissants, maybe, or Danish. Did he even like that kind of stuff? Maybe he was the bacon and eggs type. She didn't know much about him.

The coffee maker gurgled to a stop. Finny was pouring a cup when the pieces fell into place. The old woman, Leila. It was her friend, the one who'd been killed, who was talking about huckleberries. What a weird coincidence.

She slid the carafe back onto the machine and picked up her cup. What had the old woman said? Her friend had called for somebody—a bird's name and what? Finny strained to remember the words, how they'd sounded in the old lady's cracked voice.

" 'The huckleberries is dead.' " That's what she said.

"No." Finny took another drink of coffee. It was just a coincidence. Maybe the poor guy was remembering something from his childhood. He'd been dying, after all.

Finny stared at the kitchen counter. But he'd been running away from someone. Isn't that what old Leila said? Someone had been looking for him, and he'd run right out into the street to get away.

Finny set her cup down. Elliot was dead, Julia, too. Her house had been searched, and someone out there believed she had a manuscript she'd never seen. How crazy was it to think there might be some connection between that manuscript and Leila's friend?

It couldn't hurt to check.

Finny put on her shoes and gathered up purse and keys. She was on her way out the back door to the garage when she hesitated. Chris would worry if he called and she was gone. But she was only going three blocks, and odds were she'd be back before he called. She shut the door behind her and hurried to the garage.

The wind spat mean little pellets of snow against the windshield as she backed out of the garage and waited for the door to close. She drove out of the alley and headed for Leila's rest home, not noticing the silver Olds that pulled out from the middle of the block to follow her.

INTERLUDE

*L*arkspur's hand clawed at the mound of dirt and gravel in front of him. He closed his eyes and felt the rocks trail past his cheek.

Couldn't breathe. Must have broken his ribs when they kicked him.

Two young punks he didn't even know. Should've known they was there. He'd heard 'em, he'd felt 'em. He should've gone on and come back later for his stash. They got everything, bending over his stuff like vultures, figuring out how much dope they could get with it. Larkspur coughed, and pain grabbed at his guts.

The wind dropped down the side of the mound and skimmed between his back and his shirt. The temperature was dropping fast. Without his coat he was dead if it froze tonight. He stretched his arm up again to see if he could grab hold of something. The movement made him cough, and he could taste blood in the back of his throat.

The drone of the crane on the other side of the bridge hummed in his ears. If he could get to the top of this pile, maybe somebody could see him.

The muscles in his thin arms tightened as he reached upward again. His nails scratched over the gravel, and he jackknifed one leg to push his body higher. Sharper pain bit into his middle as the gravel gave way. He slid farther down the pile, stones scraping against the side of his face. He rolled onto his back and stared at the bridge looming over him.

The cough started deep in his gut and swept up through his chest. He levered himself onto his side in time for the blood to gush out of his mouth. It soaked through the round stones of the gravel. Larkspur felt a hard, cold kernel of panic inside. He didn't want to die all alone.

CHAPTER

16

*T*he wind whistled through the empty metal chairs on the front porch of the rest home. Finny ran up the steps and pounded on the door. After a moment, the woman she'd seen that afternoon opened it.

"Why, hello."

"I'm sorry to bother you, but would it be possible to talk to Leila?"

She pulled the door open wider. "Come in, it's freezing." The door stuck, and she had to push it shut. "Let's go to my office; it's just around the corner." She led Finny past the hulking Coke machine and into a faded cubicle, its tired walls hung with travel posters.

"Now." She closed the door. "What's this about, Miss—"

"Sorry. My name is Finny Aletter."

"Sarah Jane Mallory."

Finny nodded. "You're going to think I'm crazy, but Leila said something this afternoon that made me think that her friend, the one who was killed last night, might have been involved in something very dangerous." Finny told her about the Twain manuscript. "Whoever has it is extremely vulnerable. I can't imagine what the selling price would be, but I do know that it's enough to have caused one—maybe two—deaths. If Leila's friend had it, then it's possible he was killed for it as well."

"You really think there might be a connection?"

"I know it sounds crazy, but I think it's worth checking with Leila to see."

Sarah Jane's crystal eyes clouded. "The only problem is, she's been medicated. We had a hard time settling her down this evening, so I gave her lithium."

"She's unconscious?"

"Oh, no. It's just that I can't guarantee she'd be any help. She might not even remember what she told you. If you could come back tomorrow, I'm sure she'll be able to help you."

Finny thought of the whisperer on the telephone. "If it would be harmful to her, I'll wait, but if I could just try . . ."

Sarah Jane nodded. "Let me see how she is. She was watching TV a few minutes ago. Maybe she can help." She slipped out the door and was back in a few moments. "I sent for her; she'll be here in a minute. Don't expect much, and talk to her gently. She was really upset earlier."

Finny nodded.

There was a rap on her door and a man, his drooping face puzzled, leaned in to report. "Leila's not in the TV room, Sarah Jane."

"She must've gone to her room. Thanks, Les." Sarah Jane

smiled over her shoulder at Finny. "I'll run up and see if she feels like talking to you. Have a seat."

"Thanks."

A few minutes later, Sarah Jane was back, a frown between her light brows. "She's not in her room. Hold on a minute. I'll look for her. She's got to be around here somewhere."

But after a while, it was clear she wasn't. Sarah Jane, with a number of the other residents helping her, searched the entire house. Leila was gone.

Sarah Jane was calling the police when Finny left.

The powdery snow that had sifted over everything glitzed into rhinestones in the rays of the street light outside the rest home. Finny walked the half block to her car and got in. When she turned on the headlights, they shone on Leila, leaning against the rear fender of the car ahead of Finny's. In her worn coat, the long skirt of her flannel nightgown hanging below it, with her white hair trailing over her shoulders, Leila was a force to be reckoned with.

Finny scrambled out of the car. "Where the hell did you spring from?" Leila stood passive under Finny's hands. "Did you know Sarah Jane was looking for you? She's calling the cops right now."

Leila just looked at her. "I heard what you said. About my Bennie."

A chill unrelated to the cold went up Finny's spine. "When—you mean when Sarah Jane and I were talking?"

"I heard what you said."

Finny's arm settled around Leila's shoulders. "I'm sorry, Leila. I don't even know if what I told Sarah Jane is true. I'm just trying to find out about a manuscript—a book that some people want."

"You take me to Larkspur."

Finny peered into her face. She'd mentioned a Larkspur this afternoon. "I don't understand."

"Bennie, he found him a box—a nice wood box. He was gonna sell it so we could have a new start." She reached into her pocket and pulled out a Swiss Army knife, the spear blade extended. "Larkspur give him this for the papers in the box."

"So this Larkspur has the papers now?"

"You said them papers was valuable."

"Yes." Snow was falling again. Finny pulled the edges of Leila's coat together over her nightgown and fastened the buttons that remained. "Let's get you back inside before you freeze." She grasped Leila's arm. "Come on—"

"You take me to see Larkspur."

Finny's hand stilled at the low command. "Tomorrow. I'll take you to see him tomorrow."

"Now. I know where he keeps his treasures."

"You know I can't take you there now, Leila. It's late and snowing, and you—"

Leila raised the knife and held it, point up, within striking distance of Finny's chin. "Now."

Finny gaped at her. She'd been treating Leila like a child. The kid had grown up.

"Larkspur took what belonged to Bennie."

All she had to do was run. Leila was too slow to do anything to stop her. Finny glanced down at the knife, wavering now in the puffy fingers.

"Okay, I'll take you."

*   *   *

Leila stared out the side window of the car. "Turn here."

The street approached the old Eighth Avenue viaduct, then stopped, blocked off by a ROAD CLOSED sign in the middle of it.

"Go around the sign," Leila said.

"You sure my car can get through here?" Finny looked at the construction equipment clustered around the supports of the bridge.

"Go up a little yonder." Leila pointed past the sign. "The road goes in farther."

Finny's little car eased around the sign and went to the end of the pavement. The tires bumped over the washboard dirt road that petered out beside railroad tracks, where gravel and dirt were piled in mounds about ten feet high. Finny braked in front of two traffic barriers. Their orange blinking lights made the mounds look as though they were moving.

Leila opened the passenger door and shifted her bulk out of the car.

"Wait a minute." Finny was regretting going along with this. "I don't think we ought to get out. You had that medicine and all—" The door slammed on her words.

Finny stuffed her handbag under the driver's seat and turned off the headlights. As she left the car, the cold wind eddied around, flinging the resurgent snow at her. She took a quick look at the huge old bridge looming overhead, and snow fell between her neck and the collar of her shirt.

The bridge stretched across the shadowed railroad yards and the attendant buildings strung throughout the lowlands near the South Platte River. The lonely light at the end of the pavement lit one tower support that soared into the shadows above her like the leg of a concrete Colossus.

Leila was halfway to the darkness under the bridge. Finny

started after her, then darted back to the car. She'd just as soon bed down in a haunted house as wander around under that bridge without a flashlight. As the door swung open, she thought she heard something behind her. She whirled around, heart pounding, and peered into the darkness that moved with the throb of the warning lights.

She waited for a moment, listening, then reached inside for her flashlight. It was just her nerves. This little adventure was on a par with going through a graveyard on Hallowe'en night. The solid metal cylinder of the flashlight was comforting in her hand. She slammed the car door shut and hurried to catch up with Leila, her breath clouding the chill air.

Their footsteps crunched in the gravel under the unused bridge. The pressure of the wind died and passed into quiet.

"It's around here someplace," Leila said suddenly.

Finny looked quickly around her, fighting back the impulse to hush her. She felt they should be very quiet.

Leila's side-to-side gait was steady on the uneven ground. "Bennie followed Larkspur here one time." She grunted as she climbed a small rise in the ground.

Finny was shivering with more than the cold. It was so unearthly isolated here. The distant sounds of traffic were the only reminders that there was a city around this spot.

The ground was uneven in the elongated circle of the flashlight as they passed into the gloom cast by the bridge. Finny tripped and fell to her hands and knees. The flashlight landed beside her, shining at nothing. The stinging of her palms triggered a brief flash of childhood, of falls from roller skates and bicycles, when scraped skin was the only failure known. She got up and, without thinking, spat on her palms and blew against the hurt.

Behind her was the sound of shifting gravel.

"Did you hear that?" There was no answer. Finny turned and saw Leila at least ten yards away, near more mounds of gravel.

Finny scooped up the flashlight and swung it around in a circle, holding it at the end of her straightened arm like a weapon. There was nothing to see but the dirt road and the piles of gravel.

Finny's hand crept over her heart. It was leaping like Baryshnikov in a solo. She took a deep breath and turned on her heel to stride over the rough ground to Leila. "We've got to leave." She tried to catch her breath. "We're not going to find anything in the dark."

Leila ignored her. Her pale skin was orange, then gray as the light from the traffic barrier blinked off and on. She was sidling around one of the bridge supports. She stroked the surface of the rough concrete with her fingers as if reading Braille.

Finny shone the flashlight over the support. The hole in the concrete was the size of a saucer, with cracks radiating from its edges like the filaments of a spider's web.

A groan came from behind her.

Finny froze. Her dream about Elliot flashed through her mind and, for a moment, she couldn't move. Then she jerked into motion and, before she could think about it, went toward the sound, behind the mounds of gravel.

The white circle of light from her flashlight bounced over the hill of dirt and rock. Finny, walking as quietly as she could, stopped at the bottom of the hill and listened. There was a scrabbling sound of rock against rock, then only the breath of a breeze.

Finny heard footsteps behind her and spun round. Leila

was at her heels. Finny's breath came out in a gust, and she turned back to the pile of gravel.

She walked around the base, but the gravel had flowed against a wall of brick and poured concrete. There was no way around it. The scraping sound came again. "I'm going to check behind here."

Finny started up the hill of gravel, her feet sliding down the loose stuff with each step she took. Pebbles slid into one of her tennis shoes and lodged under her toes.

She was panting when she got to the top, and she had to steady herself with a hand against the rough mix of gravel and dirt. She pointed the flashlight down the other side. The light skittered over the slope to the bottom of the hill, and the man lying there on his back.

"What is it?" Leila was nearly to the top.

"There's someone down there."

The gravel shifted as Leila moved her way ponderously to Finny's side. She stopped at the summit to peer down the shaking beam of light, then waded down. "It's Larkspur. Jesus almighty."

Finny half fell in her wake and skidded to a stop just short of the man's body. The flashlight beam showed his wounds all too clearly. Both cheeks were scraped raw; small bits of gravel were in them. His cracked lips were nearly black with dried blood. He was still alive.

Leila eased his head onto her lap, crooning to him.

Finny began to think again. "Don't move him. We've got to call an ambulance."

"Lord, Lord, look at his ribs." Leila had unbuttoned Larkspur's filthy shirt and pulled it open. The skin over his ribs was deep purple. Finny's eyes widened in horror at the sight of the jagged edge of one rib poking through his skin.

"Cover him up," Finny told her. "We've got to keep him warm." She slid out of her corduroy parka and knelt to tuck it around the man's upper body. "Can you stay here with him while I go for help?"

Leila stroked Larkspur's matted hair back from his forehead. "You go."

"You have to stay right here with him," Finny said. "He has to be kept warm."

Leila nodded. "You go."

Larkspur groaned and moved his hand from side to side. His lips moved, but they couldn't hear what he said.

Finny stood up. "I'll find the nearest phone and come back as soon as I've called for help. Just stay here and wait for me, okay?"

Leila nodded again.

"Finn!" Larkspur's eyes were open, focused on Leila. "Five thousand. The boy said . . . that much."

Finny handed the flashlight to Leila. "Take this. I'll be back as fast as I can."

Finny clambered up the gravel slope. In her mind she was away to the car already. The gas station they'd passed on Eighth Avenue was still open. She reached the top of the mound and half slid down the other side.

The wind took fresh heart and gusted through the supports of the old bridge. Finny ran across the ground. She was shaking with cold, her jeans and sweater vanquished by the wind.

A hand shot out from the bridge support and jerked her into the shadows.

Finny was sent sprawling. A flashlight beam shone in her eyes.

"Where're you going, Finny?" It was the whisper she'd heard on the phone. "Where's your friend?"

Finny fought for breath. "Get that light out of my face."

"So you can see me?" The malice in the breathy voice made Finny even more afraid. "It won't do you any good."

Finny scrambled to her feet. "What do you want?" She tried to make the words strong, but she was shaking so much her voice wavered.

"Where's the manuscript, Finny?"

Finny bit back a sob. "I don't know."

"I don't believe you."

"Look." Finny's voice was shaking as much as the rest of her. "I never had it."

The figure seemed to grow larger. "I've followed every false lead there is trying to find the damned thing. You're the only one who could have it."

His voice slipped in and out of the whisper as his anger grew. She knew that voice.

"It's a matter of life and death." He laughed and Finny had it. Jon Darrow.

She took a step backward. If she could run for help . . .

"Stop moving, Finny. I have a gun and I'll use it. I'm not kidding."

"Right." Sweat dripped into her eyes. "I saw what you did to the old man. If I had the manuscript, I'd give it to you."

"Don't try to feed me some line." He stepped toward her menacingly. "You and Elliot were always tight. But you were smart enough to take the goodies for yourself. Don't expect me to be the kind of fool Elliot was. There isn't anyone left who could have it!"

"There has to be."

"Jesus." Darrow's voice cracked. "I've been on a fucking merry-go-round. Elliot promised me—*promised me*—if I'd make the connections, he'd split the profit. Then he's dead. I'm into the big boys for almost a quarter of a million, and he's dead."

His shadow pulsated across the ground toward Finny. "Julia didn't have it. She would've given it to me before I— she would've given it to me. Stupid little bitch."

Finny heard the sound, a scraping, and pushed back the fear. "I came here to look for it." She raised her voice. "There's a man who—"

The shadow figure behind Darrow hit him at knee level, and his gun went off. His head thudded against the base of the bridge support as he fell.

Leila pushed herself onto her knees and hammered on him, right then left, "You killed him," she screeched. "You killed my Bennie."

17

*B*efore she could move, footsteps thudded past Finny. A few seconds later, Leila was still.

"Leave her alone," Finny yelled. She stumbled toward the figure bending over the shadows at the base of the bridge support. "Leave her alone."

"Hold it," a voice snapped from behind her. "Don't move."

Finny stopped, confused. "What—"

"Police." A flashlight clicked on, and she was squinting at the uniformed officer patting her down with one hand. He tugged her around by one shoulder. Thin-faced, young, he was keyed up, on the alert. "Where's the gun?"

Finny lifted her hand to point toward Jon Darrow.

"Easy," the cop cautioned. "Ray," he called over his shoulder, "did you find the gun?"

The other cop's flashlight was bobbing over Leila and Jon

Darrow, still as death on the ground. The beam of light froze. "Yeah. Here it is."

Beside him, Leila said something Finny couldn't hear. The cop, towering over her, held her arm in support as she limped to Finny, her hair blowing around her head in the wind.

The young cop aimed the flashlight at each of them in turn. "What's been goin' on here?"

"There's a man," Finny managed through chattering teeth, "hurt badly—behind the gravel over there. He needs an ambulance."

"Larkspur's dead," Leila said.

The first cop glanced at his partner. "I'll go take a look. You come with me," he said to Finny.

"Make it fast," Ray said. "I'll radio the medics soon as you're back."

Finny and the cop climbed up the gravel hill together. Leila had left Finny's jacket tucked around Larkspur's neck as if he were asleep. In the white beam of the flashlight, his face was gray under the dusting of snow, his livid cheeks veiled. The glitter of his half-open eyes had hope flaring in Finny for an instant.

The cop's fingers were on Larkspur's neck. After a moment, he let them drop and shook his head. He got to his feet. "This your coat?" At Finny's nod, he started to pull it away from the body.

"Leave it," Finny said.

"Won't do him any good now."

"Leave it." She couldn't help but think Larkspur would be cold without it.

"How'd you get here so fast?" Finny asked the cop as they walked back.

"We've been tailing Darrow since late this afternoon, and he's been following you."

"Thank God."

They walked through the thickening snow to the patrol car.

After that, it was a question of waiting. Finny and Leila shared the blanket the tall cop got out of the trunk. The old woman was passive, her vengeful outburst gone behind the emptiness in her eyes. The old, sad child was back and who could blame her? A rest home didn't look so bad after a night like this. "I'm sorry, Leila."

Leila looked out the window at the snow. "Bennie's dead. Larkspur, too. Got to be with Larkspur, not with Bennie."

Finny patted her hand, the skin soft and doughy as rising bread. "I'm sure it was a comfort to Larkspur to have you with him at the end."

"Didn't know me. Said something about money, five thousand, he said, and told me to tell the boy." Her pudgy fingers pleated the rough blanket.

"He must have had the manuscript—you know, the papers Bennie found." At Leila's silence, Finny went on. "Remember, you heard me tell Sarah Jane about it earlier."

Leila continued as if she hadn't heard. "Said it was his pa's, he wanted the five thousand, and then he died." Her eyes didn't move from the window.

The flash of red and blue lights stirred the shadows surrounding the bridge, then an ambulance was bumping over the dirt road.

The paramedics were loading Jon Darrow into the ambulance when another police car skidded to a stop beside it. Barelli erupted from it, asked a sharp question of the paramedic. At her answer he strode to the squad car and pulled open the rear door. "Finny?" He reached in and grabbed hold of her arm, tugging her out of the car. Then he was holding her as if his arms were the only thing between her and immediate disintegration. She wasn't sure they weren't.

"Are you all right?" His voice got lost somewhere in the lower registers.

"Sure, just great." And she proved it by starting to cry.

A burst of laughter woke Finny. She opened her eyes, focusing slowly on the half-empty water cooler that hummed in the corner. Two men were walking down the hallway. One laughed again. She wondered what they could find that was so funny.

She'd fallen asleep on the gray vinyl couch outside the Homicide unit. Her arm had pillowed her head and now felt like one of the hard bolsters that protruded from either end of the couch like sausages at parade rest.

She was getting a drink of water when Barelli came out of the room down the hall. His hair was rumpled, as though he'd been pushing his fingers through it. He smiled crookedly. "How're you doing?"

She lifted one shoulder. "Okay 'til I woke up."

"We can get out of here in about an hour." At her quick glance of dismay, he ruffled her hair. "Paper work, babe." She tried for a smile, and he kissed the side of her mouth.

Finny yawned. "Did Jon say anything?"

"You mean did he confess? No. His lawyer's with him, and neither one of them is talking, yet."

Finny wadded up her empty cup and tossed it into the

wastebasket beside the cooler. "I can imagine what kind of manure they'll be spreading when they do."

"Don't worry," Barelli said. "With what Darrow said to you about Julia Simons, we can nail him. We'll find out what happened with Fulton. You want some coffee?"

Finny shook her head. "I want to go home, Chris. I'm tired out. You don't need me any more tonight, do you?" She glanced up at him. "I mean, officially."

Barelli's leer faded. "It's only a little after nine. As soon as I tango in triplicate, I'm out of here."

"So you can come to my house then. I'll fix you something to eat." His worried look was back. Finny sighed. "For Pete's sake, Chris, I just want to go home. You've got Jon Darrow. There's nothing to worry about. It's not even that far."

Barelli's eyes searched hers. "You scared me out of about ten years, you know."

"Chris, I'll be fine." Finny fought off annoyance. She'd feel the same way if their positions were reversed.

Barelli nodded. "Okay, but wait here a minute."

"Chris—" He loped down the hallway and darted through a door. He was back in seconds, carrying his topcoat. "Here, take this." He settled it around her shoulders.

"What about you? It's cold enough to freeze hell out there."

Barelli's mouth twitched. "Nah, purgatory, maybe, but not hell." His hands rested on her shoulders, and the smile he gave her had her hormones sitting up and taking notice. "Take the damn coat."

Finny tiptoed to brush his lips with hers. "Thanks."

"Chris." Eddie Apodaca was in the office doorway. His tie was loose, and he'd folded up the sleeves of his shirt, but by the expression in his eyes, he was still on duty. He nodded at Finny.

Barelli's hold on Finny's shoulders tightened, then he let her go. "I thought you went home."

"Started to. Darrow's lawyer just called from the hospital."

"What the hell did he want?"

Eddie smiled. "It seems his man wants to confide in you."

Barelli raised one brow. "Let me guess. He wants to 'cooperate with the authorities.'"

Eddie's eyes twinkled. "Aren't you sharp."

"First thing in the morning?"

Eddie shook his head. "Tonight. The sooner the better."

Barelli slanted a glance down at Finny. "I thought he was too groggy from being attacked by—what did he call her—a 'crazy old broad.'"

"Guess he got ungrogged. Amazing how bein' charged with a couple of murders will clear your mind." Eddie started folding down his shirtsleeves.

"Then we better get over there."

Eddie nodded again and went back into the office.

"Guess I won't get to your place as soon as I thought," Barelli murmured to Finny. "This could take a while."

"What does he want? You think he'll tell you what happened to Elliot?"

"He probably wants to cop a plea." Barelli cupped her cheek with one hand. "I wish he'd wait till morning."

"You'll need your coat." Finny started to shrug it off her shoulders, but Barelli tugged at both lapels.

"Keep it. There's a spare around here somewhere." He kissed her lightly on the nose. "I'll be home as soon as I can. You drive carefully."

"Okay." She waved at him from the elevator.

The streets were treacherous, black ice under the kind of snowfall that usually restricts itself to little glass domes. The wet and heavy stuff had coated the trees and was weighing down the power lines. By the time Finny reached her house, the wind was increasing, hurling flakes against the windshield. She ran quickly from the garage to the back door, fighting with the wind over the long folds of Barelli's coat.

Finny pushed the door shut and slumped against it. A glob of snow loosed itself from her hair and slid down her cheek. The hunter home from the hill, she thought tiredly. What a hell of a night. Barelli's coat slipped from her shoulders and lay among the snow and ice she'd tracked onto the floor.

She hung the coat on the rack and kicked off her boots. It was over. She ought to feel like she'd shed the proverbial millstone, Atlas throwing off the globe to go into another line of work. Instead, a little piece of her brain was still on alert, as if nudging her toward something else. Her adrenaline button was probably stuck on full speed ahead.

Finny trailed into the kitchen. They always prescribed hot, sweet coffee for shock, but that wasn't worth diddley if you were in the market for oblivion. For that you had to have scotch, or a variation thereof. Chris could have the coffee, if she got around to making any.

She poured herself a drink and walked slowly into the living room. Jon would have killed her, she had no doubts about that. If he hadn't thought she had the manuscript, she'd be out there getting snowed on like old Larkspur. And Jon would've had fun doing it. The enjoyment in his voice when he had her helpless, the way he came toward her—

She wasn't going to think about that part of it, at least not until Chris was beside her, preferably in bed, with a stack of comforters over them and all the lights on.

She plumped herself onto the sofa and tucked her legs under her. The window glass vibrated with the push of the wind and the curtains swayed. Finny shivered.

She took another drink, the scotch tingling on her tongue. Jon had hidden so much hatred behind the bluff, hearty salesman and the proud husband and father. Had there always been the split, or did greed over the Twain manuscript get out of control? *The Death of Huckleberry Finn.* More than Huck had died because of it.

Finny leaned her head on the back of the sofa, wincing at the soreness in her neck. She was lucky to be able to feel anything. Julia hadn't been so fortunate. Jon called her a stupid bitch, as if that were reason enough to kill her. She deserved to die, your honor, she was a stupid bitch. And Elliot, too. What had he said? "He's dead." Jon wasn't responsible, no sir, both Julia and Elliot brought it on themselves, he was just caught up in the ethos of the thing.

She leaned forward to put her glass on the coffee table. The message light on the answering machine glowed red. Finny switched on the machine and leaned back against the soft cushions.

"Finny, it's Linsay Tremaine. I just wanted to let you know . . . the auditor has found discrepancies in Elliot's ledgers. To the tune"—Linsay's voice cracked—"to the tune of ninety-three thousand dollars. They want to talk to us tomorrow. Especially you and me. Come in early if you can." The high-pitched signal squeaked, and the tape whirred on silently.

Finny stared at the machine as if it had attacked her. Embezzlement—Elliot? It couldn't be. He'd always stressed integrity. "Play tough but clean." Jesus, ninety-three thousand bucks.

The manuscript. Jon had kicked in some money, but Elliot needed more to buy it. Good old Elliot, a size eleven in clay shoes, narrow width. He'd cooked the books to buy that goddamned manuscript.

Finny pushed herself off the couch. She'd make that coffee now, and, if she was lucky, Chris would show up soon and maybe the coffee would be enough to make up for crying all over him. Her hand slapped against the swinging door to the kitchen.

She moved around the kitchen restlessly. It was like a curse, with every person who came into contact with the Twain manuscript losing everything just to obtain it. Elliot and Julia had paid with their lives, as had Larkspur and Leila's friend Bennie. And all for the money. Was there any one of them who had wanted it for anything but money? From the hundreds of thousands that Jon and Elliot were going for to the measly five thousand someone had promised Larkspur, that's what the Twain manuscript had been all about.

Finny tore a paper towel off the roll and wiped her cheeks. She wished she had the manuscript in her hands right now—she'd shred it and burn it and nobody else would ever be hurt by it again. The lights flickered overhead.

Grief fades, and rage as well. The body isn't designed to maintain the white heat of either. As Finny cooled down, her mind started working again. There was one thing no one had figured out yet: where was the manuscript? Of all the people who'd pursued it, from Bart Cronin to Larkspur, who had it now?

The ring of the telephone nearly brought on cardiac arrest. When she heard Barelli's voice, her heart thundered back into business.

"I wanted to check to see if you got home," he said roughly. "The roads are a nightmare."

"Where are you?"

"We just got back from the hospital. We've got Darrow on the Simons killing. There was tissue under her nails, and Darrow crumbled like rotten brick when we told him we were subpoenaing blood and skin samples from him."

"What about Elliot?"

"What? There's a lot of static on the line."

"Did he say anything about killing Elliot?" Finny said more loudly.

"He put on a song and dance." Barelli's voice was fuzzed with the rushing sound on the line. "Says he couldn't have, wouldn't have—and tossed your name around."

"What do you mean?"

"He says you killed—" The phone went dead.

Finny clicked the plunger a few times, with no response. The lines were probably down. On the thought, the lights flickered again.

She replaced the receiver. What was Jon saying, that she killed Elliot? How like him, to try to bluster his way out of it. If he'd admitted to killing Julia, then what did he have to lose by telling the truth about Elliot?

She started to make coffee, her hands working automatically as she thought about Jon Darrow. His desperate frustration out at the bridge, following her to get the manuscript. He'd put money into it, a lot of money. "Elliot promised me . . . split the profits . . . he's dead."

Finny dropped the coffee scoop back into the can. The

only way Jon stood to gain anything from the Twain manuscript was if Elliot resold it. For Jon to kill him before the transaction was complete was crazy. Unless it was some kind of double cross—but Jon was furious because Elliot "was dead."

"My God," Finny whispered. If Jon didn't kill Elliot, then this whole thing wasn't over yet.

The lights faded out, then came on again.

Finny pulled open a drawer and rummaged for candles. She found matches and sat down at the kitchen table. Everything still revolved around the Twain manuscript. If she could just figure out where it was . . .

Leila had waved the knife in her face, the knife she said Larkspur gave Bennie for the old papers. And Larkspur had died talking about a boy and five thousand dollars. Something else Leila said, something about his pa. Tell the boy, it's his pa's, Larkspur wanted the five thousand dollars.

Finny stared at the table, not liking the way the pieces were coming together.

The boy. "Said it was his pa's." Larkspur's dying words according to Leila, in her grandmotherly voice while they waited in the police car. His pa's. His father's. The manuscript was his father's, and he would pay five thousand dollars to get it back.

Richard Fulton.

Jenn was afraid of him and had told Cronin she thought he might have killed Elliot. Finny's stomach turned at the thought of Larkspur's battered face. Richard had a violent temper and was erupting with hostility toward everyone. Could he have killed Elliot and Larkspur? He'd called Finny one of Elliot's women, and the hate in his voice had frightened her badly.

Chris needed to know about this. She got up to try the phone, but it was still dead. Finny hung up and looked around the room in frustration. When would he be coming? He said he was back at headquarters.

He also said the roads were a nightmare. God, what if he decided to stay there?

The lights went out. Finny waited a moment to see if they'd come back on, but they didn't.

She groped toward the table and found the candles. The match flared brightly in the dark room, and she held the flame to the wicks.

The lights would come back on, and Chris would be knocking on the door before she knew it. They could use the radio in his car to call headquarters.

Ten minutes later Finny knew she couldn't wait any longer. If Richard had killed any or all of those people, what was to keep him from killing again? If he wanted to hurt Jennifer and Marian, who would stop him?

The snow plows hadn't gotten to Speer yet, and Finny's car tended to slide. Springtime in the Rockies. Fretting at her mind like a dripping faucet was how Chris would feel when he got to her house and found her gone. She'd tried the phone one more time before she left, then scrawled a note for him, leaving it tacked on the front door. It was a case of a woman's gotta do what a woman's gotta do. What other choice did she have?

The real issue was what to do when she got to the Fulton

house. Presumably Richard was there. Just as presumably, she was the last person he'd want to see. If she could convince Marian and Jennifer to come back home with her, then the cops could take care of him at their leisure, always assuming he stuck around for the process. The way her luck had gone lately, it wasn't going to be that easy.

Finny pulled up in front of the Fulton house. Lights were on on both the first and second floors, shining through the mullioned windows, each little square frosted with snow, like an illustration from Currier and Ives.

Finny pushed the doorbell. Please, please, she was saying to herself, bracing herself against the pushy wind, feeling her palms sweat. Let me get through this.

The door swung open and she was face to face with Richard Fulton.

Her brain made a lightning survey of the options open to her: she could turn on her heel and scuttle back to her car; she could claim to be selling magazines and pick up a few extra bucks; she could fake it.

"Hello, Richard," she said calmly and walked through the door. "I'd like to talk to your mother."

Richard Fulton, unshaven, eyes red-rimmed, pivoted, one hand still on the doorknob. "Get out of here," he said thickly. Finny didn't have to look at the glass in his hand to know he'd been drinking.

"It's important," Finny said. She put a mental hand over the part of her that was gibbering with nerves. "Is she here?"

"Richard, close the door, for heaven's sake." Jenn, arrested in mid-step, met Finny's eyes from the hall. She was demure in lavender wool slacks and white cashmere sweater, but her eyes glittered like mica under the sun. "Well, well," she said, strolling into the foyer, "so you've finally decided to deal."

Behind her, Richard closed the door.

Finny looked back and forth between the two of them. Everybody always says you learn the most from your mistakes. She had the feeling she was in for a postgraduate degree.

CHAPTER

18

*I*t wasn't just a family gathering. Bart Cronin ambled into the foyer from the hallway. "What are you doing here so late, Finny?"

A piece of Finny's mind noted his patterned burgundy ascot, at odds with the naked calculation in his eyes. Mismatched accessories were so tacky. "I want to talk to Marian."

"And whatever Finny wants, Finny gets." The malice in Richard's singsong words was in his face, too, his pale eyes narrowed, his thin lips twisted. He raised his glass to her, slopping clear liquid over the side. Finny's stomach lurched at the sight of his knuckles: they were scraped and bruised. "You assume we'll trot off to get Mother like good little children, don't you?" He took a step toward her, and Finny's nerve endings sounded an alarm. "Mother can't see you right now, bitch."

231

"For God's sake, Richard." Jennifer eyed him with distaste. "If you can't control yourself, go sleep it off. If you'll remember, we have some business to conduct." Finny could almost hear the switch click with the smile Jenn turned on her. "Come into the living room, Finny."

"No." Richard's smart-aleck hostility dropped off him like icicles off the eaves of a house. "Finny goes. Now."

Bart Cronin maintained his friendly air, but he moved closer to Jennifer. "It won't take long, Richard. I'm sure Finny won't outstay her welcome."

Finny would be out of here like a rocket from a launcher as soon as she saw Marian, she thought grimly. "Where's your mother?" she asked Jennifer.

"Come on, Finny, I'm all grown up now," Jenn said impatiently. "Bart told me about the Twain manuscript and, thanks to Richard, I know all about you and Daddy. Let's cut the crap and get down to business."

"What business?"

Jenn shot a can-you-believe-it look at Cronin. "The manuscript, of course. We know you've got it."

Of their own volition, Finny's eyes sought out Richard Fulton. Shoulders against the wall, one leg bent, he was watching her. "No, I don't have it."

"The game's over." Jenn's hand fastened onto Finny's arm, and she pulled her around in a swift movement. "Damn you, *where is it?*"

Cronin reached for her. "Jenn, settle down, this isn't—"

"No!" Jenn twisted away from his hands. The face she turned to Finny was fierce with anger, hatred darkening the wide green eyes. "Everything's gone—the money, the house, everything. All because of that fucking manuscript. I don't care what you were to Daddy. He wouldn't want you to have what's mine."

"Yours, little sister?" Richard said softly. "Yours?"

Jenn's gaze jerked back to him. "Ours," she said breathlessly. "I meant ours." She looked at Finny again, her hand tightening on Finny's arm. "You don't have any right to it."

Finny's mind clicked through a series of images, as rapidly as a slide projector, as fleeting as the flashes of a strobe light: the child Jennifer, innocent eyes, the trust of a held hand, the solemnity of confidences exchanged over ice cream. All obliterated by the demanding stranger pulling at her arm in greed.

On a surge of anger, Finny jerked herself free. "Get this through your head," she said in a low, thick voice. "I have never had the manuscript. I don't have it now."

"Jesus, Finny," Cronin began, "do you expect—"

"Ask Richard where it is," Finny said thickly. She glanced again at Richard's raw knuckles. "Ask him about the manuscript."

Richard straightened. "What are you getting at?"

Finny's mind raced feverishly. If she could get to Marian and call the police . . . "The five thousand dollars," she said. "You promised the old man, Larkspur, you'd give it to him for the manuscript."

Richard's eyes widened, and he took a quick step toward her, but Jennifer had been following Finny's words like a cat watches its prey, and she plunged furiously between them. "You found it?" She crossed the small foyer in a rush, Cronin behind her. "Damn you to hell, you give it to me!"

Finny moved swiftly into the hallway. Marian had to be in the greenhouse. She ran to its french doors and whipped one open. It closed silently behind her and she leaned against it, breathing heavily.

Marian glanced up from the pot she was holding under the faucet. In her stained sweatshirt and jeans she looked almost as young as her daughter. "Finny? What are you doing here?"

Finny walked farther into the muggy, fecund air. The walls were alive with plants. "Marian, I need you to come with me, right now. It's very important. We need to get the police."

Marian cocked her head and a lock of light hair trailed against her cheek. "What are you talking about?"

"Oh, God." Quick, how do you convince a mother, in twenty words or less, that her son is a killer? "Just come with me. We'll be right back. *Please*, Marian."

Marian shrugged her narrow shoulders in puzzlement. "You're not making any sense."

"Listen," Finny said rapidly, "Richard's involved in a murder—an old man who had the manuscript—and he might hurt you. Marian, please come with me. We'll go out the back and—"

One of the french doors hit the wall, and the heavy greenhouse air splintered with the sound of shattering glass. Richard Fulton stood in the doorway, glaring at Finny, rage hot in his eyes. "You just love to cause trouble, don't you?" His voice was trembling, almost as if he were on the edge of tears. "You just can't leave us alone."

"Richard," Marian said, "what's happening here?"

Richard took a step toward Finny. "She never could leave us alone, Mother." His eyes were on Finny. "Everything was her fault."

Finny's gaze was held by the turbulence of his eyes, but her words were for Marian. "He killed an old man, Marian. Beat him to death for the manuscript. Look at his hands."

"Dammit, no!" Richard looked down at his hands and back at Finny in confusion. "He ran into the street—"

Finny met his eyes sickly. He had been the one pursuing Bennie.

"Mama, he's got the manuscript." Jennifer leaned against the doorjamb, one hand to her face. "He's going to keep it for himself." She let her hand drop from the vivid patch of red on her cheek.

Marian looked back and forth between the two of them. "I don't understand. You have the Twain manuscript?" she asked Richard. "You found it?"

"Where is it?" Cronin was beside Jennifer. One arm was around her shoulders, but his craggy face was flushed with excitement.

"I don't have it!" Richard turned to Marian abruptly, his lean body tense. "And I didn't kill anybody. A car hit him. And then, Mom, I found another old man named Larkspur and he said he had it. I was supposed to meet him this afternoon, but he never showed up."

"You're lying," Jenn said. "Mom," she appealed to Marian, "he wants it all for himself."

"Stop it." Marian, pale and tight-lipped, stared down her daughter. "Let him tell us."

"And you'll believe him." Jenn's eyes filled with tears. "You'll believe whatever he tells you, just because it's him telling you." She turned her face into Cronin's shoulder. "I know he has it. I know he does."

"Shut up!" Richard's face was suffused with color. "You're the one," he said to Finny. "You have it, don't you, and you're just trying to cover your ass."

Finny's muscles tightened under his stare. "How did you hurt your hand?"

Richard glanced down at his hand again. "You damned troublemaker," he said as he came toward her. He gave off waves of anger, like an enraged animal, his face twisted with hatred.

Finny backed away from him. Wrong question, she thought crazily. You asked the wrong question.

"You never would leave us alone. Always hanging around, mooning over my father."

Finny's heart was pumping panic through her veins. "Richard, you've been under a lot of stress." Oh, God, yes, if he killed his father. She took another step back. "You can get help. A lawyer, psychiatric counseling. But if you hurt me, it'll be even worse." She stopped short, her shoulder against one of the plant shelves, her eyes going to the frozen tableau behind Richard. "Stop him," she urged Cronin. "What's wrong with you?"

"You bitch, you lousy bitch." Richard swung his arm and caught Finny across the side of the face, and then she was falling against the shelves behind her and the sounds of dirt and glass and pots and Marian's voice were falling all together over her as she dropped to the floor.

It was the sound of laughter that made Finny realize that she hadn't lost consciousness.

"Mother?" The raging man was gone. Richard Fulton stood flat-footed, looking down at her, his face blank and childlike, nothing written on it but disbelief. No, he wasn't looking at her. His eyes were on the debris beside her, the dirt, broken clay pots, the black barrel of the pistol that jutted from the jagged-edged pot beside her arm.

Finny's eyes wandered over the gun, noting the dirt on it, moist clumps adhering to the deadly metal shape of it. She looked up past the shock in Richard's face to the woman behind him.

Marian pushed the errant lock of hair off her cheek. "You always were the clumsiest child," she murmured softly to Richard. "You always were."

Finny moved and dislodged a pile of debris that slid out onto the tile floor. With the soft whisper of dirt, Jennifer began to cry in loud, ugly sobs.

Marian turned and walked to the sink, her movements heavy and slow like those of an old woman. She pulled the faucet handle toward her and put her hands under the gushing water.

"Mother." Richard moved closer to her. "Mother."

Finny lifted one hand to the pain that throbbed in her left cheek. Her eyes remained on Marian.

"Mother, please." Richard turned her toward him, paying no attention to the water dripping from her hands. "You have to tell me now."

Marian looked past him into Finny's eyes. "What's the old saying? 'There's justice in the universe. No mercy, but justice.' "

Finny shook her head slowly.

"You knew, didn't you?" Marian asked Richard tenderly. "When I told you about the little man with the box, didn't you know? How did you think I knew that he had it?" She looked past him to Finny. "I didn't hate Elliot. It's just that I was so tired of being taken for granted."

Richard put his hands on her shoulders. "Are you saying you killed him, Mom? Did you kill him?"

Marian patted his cheek. "I don't expect you'll understand until you're older."

Richard's eyes were full of tears. "Mom," he said, his voice cracking, "we've got to talk—work this out somehow—I—"

Marian nodded. "I guess I knew that it would come out sooner or later."

Finny pushed herself to her feet. "Why?" She felt cold and brittle. If she bumped against anything she would break into pieces like the clay pots at her feet. Her eyes glanced off the dirt-covered gun, then returned to Marian. "Why?"

"You weren't the first," Marian said abruptly. "Nor the last. Just the one I got to know." She looked down at her wet hands.

"I tried all the advice from the women's magazines. Lacy nightgowns, new perfume." She lifted one shoulder, and her voice twisted into a parody of seduction. "Spontaneous sex." Her shoulders relaxed into defeat. "He just didn't see me anymore."

"Oh, Mama." Jennifer took a step toward her, but Marian ignored her.

"I called it a mid-life crisis and decided to weather it out." Marian came toward Finny and knelt beside the broken pot. Finny bent swiftly and moved the gun aside. Marian smiled wryly up at her, then began picking up shards of clay. "Do you know what happens to a woman with two children when she divorces? It wasn't going to happen to me. Get me that wastebasket—the one next to the counter."

Finny stared at her stupidly. When Marian glanced up at her impatiently, she moved awkwardly to do her bidding, brushing by Richard to get to the wastebasket. He didn't move. Marian dumped the pot fragments into the metal container.

Finny flinched at the loud, broken sounds.

"Economic realities," Marian continued. "That's what Elliot always said was at the heart of every problem. In our case he was right. My hands were tied, by the proverbial purse strings." Her hands moved busily among the plants and dirt and broken pots. "So, after a while, I gave up on the sexy nighties and perfumes, and tried to live with it." Her fleeting smile was wry. "Vesting my pension, you might call it."

"Jesus," Finny whispered.

"What else could I do?" Marian flared. She dropped the debris she'd accumulated and got to her feet. "I didn't know how to do anything. Elliot didn't even want me to go back to school when the kids were older. 'You're such a good hostess, a good partner,' he said. My contributions to his career should be enough." She took a deep breath, regaining control. "I knew it didn't last long with you. I could tell by the way he acted."

Finny's hands were clenched. "I'm sorry, I'm sorry."

"Oh, don't worry," Marian said contemptuously. "I didn't care about the sex part of it. That's not the most important thing, you know. You want them to _see_ you, to know who you are." Marian bit both lips and shook her head in a tight, angry movement. "I couldn't impress him. I was his partner, his hostess, but what _impressed_ him was what a mind you had for the business."

Marian looked at her. "I haven't cried in ten years, not until the funeral." She shook her head, bemused. "And then there were the others, young women who were so savvy and whose careers he was having an impact on. He didn't know what went on inside my head, and he didn't care. I was with him for thirty years, and before he died he couldn't even have told you how I spent my days. He just didn't care.

"And then the last one. Julia Simons." The name sounded like a curse on Marian's lips. "He came home early all excited and quiet and shut himself up in his study. He left his coat on the back of a chair, and I hung it up for him. The good housekeeper, the faithful servant." Her mouth twisted.

"There was a stain on the coat—I thought it needed cleaning, so I emptied the pockets, and I found the note." She laughed, a short, hateful laugh. "Right out of the soaps, don't you think?

"How long would it be, she asked him, till they could be together? Now that their love was growing inside her, she couldn't wait until they were together for all time."

Marian looked around the room in a tight, controlled movement, eyes skipping over the horrified faces of her children. "He'd knocked her up. Some kid young enough to be his daughter and she's prattling about their love and I knew I couldn't stand it anymore. I'd put my time in, and I wasn't going to be done out of my share by some kid too stupid to use birth control.

"He was in there, in his study, and I knew that he was thinking how to do it, the cheapest, quickest way he could dump me."

Marian's voice lowered, as if she were talking to herself. "So I got the gun that belonged to my father. And I went to the study and I showed Elliot the gun and I told him what I was going to do." She laughed and Finny's blood chilled at the hatred in it.

"My God, you wouldn't believe what a difference it made. For the first time in years he really saw me."

Marian's eyes met Finny's. "You have no idea how good it felt. I wasn't just a part of the scenery any more. He hung on my every word. All because of that." She motioned toward the gun on the floor.

Finny tried to swallow, but her mouth was too dry.

"I told him why I was going to do it. After all the years of accepting the humiliation, I wasn't going to be thrown away like so many of the women I know. They put in years and they put up with so much and then their husbands dump them. They end up alone and without enough money. And everyone knows they've been thrown away, onto the trash heap. Not me." She swung her head from side to side. "Not me.

"It was so flattering, the way he listened. He hadn't been that attentive since before we were married. It brought back a lot of memories." Marian's eyes looked inward. "I almost didn't go through with it, but I knew if I backed out, it would spoil it. He would never take me seriously again." Her eyes sought Finny's. "You know. If you threaten and then don't carry it out, you lose all your credibility."

Finny nodded.

Marian closed her eyes. "So I shot him. Before he could talk me out of it. It was worth it to get his attention one last time."

Jennifer, held tightly in Cronin's arms, whimpered.

"But the manuscript." Finny felt as though she were wandering in a nightmare landscape. "Everyone was looking for the manuscript."

Marian laughed. "I didn't find out what it was until Bart told me. It was on Elliot's desk, and it just came to me—how I could make it work for me. There had to be footprints into the house, you see." Her eyes lifted to Finny. "The police might think it was burglary, and they'd see the footprints." She shook her head wearily. "I ran and got Elliot's coat—it was still wet from the rain, and put it over me, over my head." A delicate frown drew her brow together. "I ran to the alley and put the box in a trash can and came back."

Marian's frown deepened. "I had it all worked out. I slid my feet to lengthen the footprints, and I took off my shoes when I got to the french doors, but then I found the glove." She looked up again into Finny's eyes. "When I slipped off Elliot's coat a glove fell from the pocket, and I put it back, but the other one wasn't there. I was running out of time, and the other glove wasn't there. I thought maybe it's in the alley and put my shoes back on and ran back. I saw the little man under the alley light with his shopping cart full of cans. He looked like a character from a children's book with his long red muffler, standing there holding the box. I couldn't look for the glove at all."

"It was at the office," Finny said numbly.

Marian smiled her strange, sad smile. "I ran back through the yard and put Elliot's coat and hat back on the chair. And then I came out here and planted the gun. Literally." Her voice caught in a low chuckle. "A pun of sorts, don't you think? If it hadn't been for you, the gun would still be fertilizing my pothos. They're called 'devil's ivy,' you know." She laughed again. "You know the ironic part? Elliot hocked everything he had to get the Twain manuscript, so I end up with nothing after all."

Finny started to speak and had to clear her throat. "You chased the man into the street," she said to Richard. "The one who picked up the box."

"I found him," Richard said faintly. "He always wore that long, red muffler. He kept talking about the box, and I couldn't get him to understand." His face tightened with frustration. "I asked him about the papers, but all he said was some bullshit about Larkspur trading him a knife, all this _bullshit_"—he looked up at Finny in anger—"and I thought he was lying. He got scared and ran away from me."

"So then you found Larkspur?" Finny asked.

"He was around a lot," Richard said. "Most of the bums knew him, knew where he hung out. He wanted five thousand dollars for the manuscript, but he never showed up this afternoon. I don't know if he really had it or not."

"How did you hurt your hands?" Finny asked gently.

She could barely hear him when he answered. "I went to get my car when Jenn left it at your house. She didn't close the door all the way, so the light was on and the battery went dead. I scraped my knuckles against the housing when I took it to get it recharged." He turned abruptly to his mother. "Oh, God, Mom, what do we do now?"

"We go down to police headquarters," Chris Barelli said from the doorway, "and start sorting through the mess. I got your note," he said to Finny.

She nodded.

A uniformed officer came through the doorway and went to Marian's side. Richard Fulton stumbled to her.

"Read her her rights," Barelli said, "and take her out to the living room. I'll be right out."

"Wait a minute," Finny said. They looked at her, Jenn at Cronin's side, Marian and Richard, the cop between them. Barelli walked toward her quickly and put one arm around her shoulders. She took a deep breath and tried to steady her voice. "The Twain manuscript. Where is it?" They all stared at her blankly, and she fought against the anger welling up inside. "How many people got killed for it—three, four? Where the hell is it?" Her voice got caught between a sob and a laugh and Barelli's arm tightened. "Where's the manuscript?"

EPILOGUE

*T*he night was quiet around the old Eighth Avenue viaduct. The snow stopped, the wind died, and the only sound nearby was the click of the orange emergency lights. Off and on.

The manuscript pages lay scattered, blown across the railroad tracks and buried in the snow.

The storm had passed, and tomorrow the snow would melt and the thick rag paper would absorb the moisture.

The angled black writing that hurried across the pages would blur as the water oozed into the ink, and the words so few had seen would bleed and dye the yellowed paper gray.

IF IT'S MURDER, CAN DETECTIVE J.P. BEAUMONT BE FAR BEHIND?...

FOLLOW IN HIS FOOTSTEPS WITH FAST-PACED MYSTERIES BY J.A. JANCE

TRIAL BY FURY	75138-0/$3.95 US/$4.95 CAN
IMPROBABLE CAUSE	75412-6/$3.95 US/$4.95 CAN
INJUSTICE FOR ALL	89641-9/$3.95 US/$4.95 CAN
TAKING THE FIFTH	75139-9/$3.95 US/$4.95 CAN
UNTIL PROVEN GUILTY	89638-9/$3.95 US/$4.95 CAN

A MORE PERFECT UNION

75413-4/$3.95 US/$4.95 CAN

DISMISSED WITH PREJUDICE

75547-5/$3.50 US/$4.25 CAN

MINOR IN POSSESSION

75546-7/$3.95 US/$4.95 CAN